ALIEN MERCENARY'S HEART

LATHAR MERCENARIES: WARBORNE

MINA CARTER

NEW YORK TIMES & USA TODAY BESTSELLING AUTHOR

CONTENTS

Chapter 1   1

Chapter 2   23

Chapter 3   39

Chapter 4   59

Chapter 5   77

Chapter 6   93

Chapter 7   109

Chapter 8   127

Chapter 9   145

Chapter 10   163

Chapter 11   181

Chapter 12   201

Chapter 13   217

Chapter 14   235

Chapter 15   249

Chapter 16   265

Chapter 17   285

Epilogue   299

About the Author   305

1

"Jesh!"

Zero jerked awake, bathed in sweat and ready to kill.

He fought his sheets blindly for a second, even as his onboard computer informed him no one was in the room. No threat, just him. With a groan, he flopped back on his bunk, breathing heavily as his bio-organics calmed down.

It was the nightmare again. The one he always had filled with fire and explosions... with pain and faces he couldn't remember. Faces distorted, the three men seemed familiar but didn't register in his memory banks. Not anywhere. Shouting, they reached for him, concern on their faces, but he couldn't hear them properly before he fell backward into darkness.

He closed his eyes and shoved his hand through the short spikes of his hair. The dream was always the same, like a memory even though he knew it wasn't. Other than that, all he knew was that the men were real, not figments of his imagination and none of them were Jesh.

The problem was, he didn't know who the fuck Jesh was, or why he screamed the guy's name.

With a groan, he hauled his ass out of his bunk and padded over to the door.

Query, he directed to his internal systems. *How long have I been asleep?*

Duration of sleep period was three hours, twenty-five minutes and seventeen seconds, the smooth voice replied in his head. It was his "other" side, the computer buried in his brain that controlled the parts of him that weren't organic. He sighed and ran his hand through his hair. Exhaustion pulled at him but there was no point staying in bed. He wouldn't sleep again.

Recommend return to sleep cycle, the onboard insisted. He silenced it with a hiss of irritation. The last thing he needed when he was running low on sleep and high on frustration was a nagging little voice in the back of his head.

The door cycled slowly, irritating him even more, and he stomped down the corridor toward the galley. It was empty. Good. With the mood he was in, he'd rip the head off his crewmates if they so much as breathed the wrong way. And for a being who could literally *hear* the biological processes of his crewmates' bodies—especially the day after curry night—the danger was genuine.

He didn't need to search the freezer unit for what he wanted. No one would dare touch his triple-chocolate caramel fudge ice cream. Not if they valued their lives.

"Oh, baby... come to daddy," he crooned, bending down to reach for it.

"Whoa! *That* was so not an image I needed! Pants, Zero. They're a thing. My mate could wander in here."

He stood, spoon already in his mouth to find Talent, the unit's newest member behind him. The tall male was sleep-rumpled, his chest bare. Scratches on his chest and dark marks around his wrist announced he was mated. Zero instantly quashed the jealousy that snuck up on him. Not because he wanted Lizzie, Tal's little human mate, but because he'd all but given up hope on any woman looking at *him* that way. What woman would want a half-machine monster?

"Is that ice cream?" Tal asked, his gaze sharpening on the tub under Zero's arm. "Chocolate?"

"No," Zero deadpanned. "It's... *iridean* squash, with... err... *cartorian* bugs. Not tasty at all."

Tal's eyebrow winged up. "You know I can read Terran. Right?"

"So?"

"The tub says 'triple choc' on the side."

Zero gave a mock-growl and sighed. "Lizzie wants chocolate?"

Talent wagged the field tin he held in his hand. "Sent me in to make field cake. She's "peckish." And it's more than my life is worth to argue with the boss. So... make with the goodies."

Zero grumbled under his breath and offered the tub. Wrapped in a thermo-sleeve, it wouldn't melt too quickly.

"Thanks, brother. She's very crabby when she's hungry."

"Hangry," Zero supplied automatically. "Humans

call it hangry. Like a cross between hungry and angry."

He had no idea how he knew that; he just did. Like so many other things, the thought arrived, fully formed, from his memory banks. And that was just typical. He could remember random, useless information, but nothing important... like what the fuck he was or where he'd come from.

"Really? They have such an odd language construction," Tal commented as he spooned ice cream into his field tin. He looked up, studying Zero suddenly. Eyes narrowing, his movements paused.

"Are you okay? You look tired... and I thought only the watch officer was up."

Zero shrugged and plonked his ass down on the bench, waiting for his ice cream back. "I can't sleep sometimes. No biggie."

"As the medical officer aboard, I'll make that decision," Talent said firmly, still spooning. Zero got worried about the level of ice cream left. How much could one tiny human woman eat? Then what the guy said registered and he looked up, shaking his head.

"Uh-uh... yeah, no. For the rest, yes. Me? No." He balanced the spoon on the end of his nose, crossing his eyes to look at it. "I'm not Lathar. Machine, remember? Don't need a medical officer. I need a mechanic."

Talent handed the ice cream tub back. Zero checked the level, and enough was left to send him into a sugar coma... for all of 2.3 seconds before his systems purged the spike.

"In that case, it's a good job I have some engineering training. Isn't it? Now talk. Or I'll go get Lizzie. *After* you put some pants on."

Zero blinked. "That's low, using your mate as a threat."

It was a viable threat. Lizzie was lovely, a genuine breath of fresh air and brightness that the entire Warborne crew had adopted immediately. But... she was relentless. If she thought there was a problem, she would not rest until she got to the bottom of it.

Within days of coming aboard, she'd cornered them all for a "getting to know you" chat. So far, T'Raal had actually been caught smiling, Red was sporting a new hair style and Skinny had learned a ditty in Terran that was so dirty it made Fin smile. Even the recalcitrant Beauty had a new plant on his bridge console.

Talent shrugged. "Whatever works. Now talk."

"I have nightmares." Zero hadn't intended to admit that, but somehow, once the words started flowing, he couldn't stop them. "It's a memory, but I don't remember it."

"What do you mean you don't remember it?" The Lathar slid into the seat opposite, his expression one of interest. "Don't you have..." he waved toward Zero's arm, "bits for that?"

"Bits? Is that the best you can do?" Zero barked a laugh. "Yeah, I have an onboard comp and memory storage."

"Really?" Talent leaned forward, studying Zero's face like he could pierce the skin with his eyes and see what lay beneath. "All cybernetic or do you still retain some percentage of organic brain matter?"

Zero shook his head. "Not all cybernetic, no. My cybernetics are integrated with my bio-organics, with approximately a sixty-forty split. Most memory functions are cybernetic, and that's the problem."

Talent shook his head, his expression blank.

"When T'Raal found me, years ago, I was damaged almost beyond repair. It took months before I could move properly and even longer before I could fight. This memory is from before then."

"Okay..."

Zero sighed and scrubbed at the top of his head. "My memory banks were blank. Completely wiped. I remembered nothing before waking up on the *Sprite*.

Yet this nightmare... the people in it... I know them. They're trying to reach me, and I'm falling... I wake screaming some guy's name. Jesh. But I don't know who the fuck they are, or who Jesh is. And it's driving me fucking crazy."

❖

"I'm sorry, Ms. Archer, but I'm afraid I don't have good news for you."

Eris Archer only kept her expression level by dint of long practice. The doctor's offices were not on her list of favorite places to be. She'd seen enough of them over the years. She knew better than to get her hopes up, but Doctor Reed's expression killed any secret hope she'd been harboring deader than a dodo.

Doctor Reed was a specialist, the best in lower limb neuro-reconstruction, which was the reason she'd hired him. She'd hoped... *prayed*... he could help her.

"Okay, Doctor. How bad is it?" Her voice was level, which she was proud of. Silly little thing to be proud of, but there you had it. In situations like this, when her very ability to walk hinged on his answer, sometimes she had to hold on to the little things.

"We have your test results back and... well, can I be frank?"

She shrugged. "You can be whoever you like, Doc."

Her attempt at humor fell flat, Reed's expression not changing.

"I'm afraid the Markovian technique will not be an option."

She nodded slowly, keeping her hands neatly folded in her lap. A veteran, she was used to being cool under fire, and her tenure as Tarantus Station Security Chief had ensured she could keep calm and professional...

Which came in real handy when all she wanted to do was scream about the unfairness of it all. She'd had so many dreams for her life, and none of them had involved being in a doctor's office having a conversation like this. But she also hadn't thought her military career would be over and she'd be forced to work for a second-rate outfit like Tarantus Station.

"We knew it was a long shot." She squashed the bitter disappointment and wondered if the doctor would offer any alternatives. Without an end to her condition in sight, she couldn't afford to pay for his services long. Not without financial help from her... yeah, she wasn't going there. *So* not going there.

She didn't glance down at her leg or the supporting brace hidden beneath her clothing. She supposed she should be grateful that exo-supports were easy to hide. None of her staff knew about her little... issue. That was the way she wanted to keep it. She didn't want whispers behind her back or the pity when they looked at her. Which was the main reason she'd told none of them about her military service.

At least the support was nothing like the archaic scaffolding of yesteryear. It ached liked a bitch, but she ignored it. She lived with pain every day. It wasn't getting any more attention just because of a little bad news.

"I'm sorry, Ms. Archer, but it's a little more complicated than that." The doctor, a small, neat little man with a dapper dress sense, regarded her steadily over the rim of his glasses. Such eyewear was unusual. Most people opted for nano-surgery to correct visual problems. Perhaps he had a condition that meant it wouldn't work?

She dragged her attention back to his words. Words she really didn't want to register because then she would have to...

"What do you mean it's a little more complicated?"

There, the words were out. The ones she hadn't wanted to voice.

The doctor's expression shifted subtly, and her heart sank. She recognized that expression. It was the standard "soften the bad news" expression common to doctors the galaxy over. Crap.

"I'm afraid the results of your last round of tests were somewhat concerning," he said gently. "The neuro-implant sites are beginning to deteriorate."

She sucked a breath in, forcing herself to remain calm. They'd told her during her initial surgery the implants would last forever. They'd lied. The devices merged to her nervous system had never been produced with longevity in mind. The manufacturers had cut corners, counting on the soldiers being dead long before the implants gave out.

"Okay," she nodded, not looking forward to another round of surgeries and mentally totting up what she had saved and how long she could afford to be in recovery. Good medical care was expensive, and she needed the best. "How long do I have? I'll have to arrange some time off for the replacement."

"I'm sorry to say it's a little more serious than

that, Ms. Archer," the doctor said, his expression grave and sympathetic. "Your implant sites have already deteriorated beyond the scope of reconstructive surgery."

She froze.

"I'm afraid once your implants fail, that will be it. You will lose the use of the limb."

Eris didn't catch the rest of the conversation as she left the doctor's office. Oh, she knew he had apologized profusely and that she'd tried to ease his concerns.... *Yes, she'd always known it was a long shot... the damage was too old... she was aware there was counseling available...* He'd tried to soothe her, saying at least she wasn't active service anymore because one more trip in a suit would finally paralyze her... but she hadn't been mentally present for any of it. Her only goal was getting the hell out of there before she could break down and scream.

Finally, she was free and clear, ducking down a side corridor. Once she was alone, away from the hustle and bustle of the station corridors, she leaned against the metal wall, closing her eyes. A single tear sneaked past her clamped eyelids. She breathed deeply, forcing the frustration and panic down.

She could do this. She *had* to. She'd known this day would come. Ever since the first of them had developed problems in the field with their armored suits, they'd all known this day would come. The day when their implants finally stopped, and they were nothing more than cripples.

She turned, her back against the metal, and leaned her head against the wall. She'd trained so long and hard to get into the Armored Infantry. To be one of the chosen few to operate a *Scorperio* portable tank suit in the field. Ironic really, that something designed to give a soldier more mobility in tough terrain would be the thing to remove hers.

Hearing footsteps coming down the corridor, she swiped quickly at her eyes and pushed upright to start walking. She nodded to the maintenance officer who hurried past, toolkit in hand. He barely looked at her, obviously intent on where he was going. Not surprisingly, something was always breaking on the station.

Continuing down the corridor, she headed for her office. Regardless of her personal situation, she still had a job to do.

For as long as she could still do it...

Her afternoon had turned into a complete and utter shitshow.

First, a group of loaders had gotten out of hand

down in the docking bay. One of the Tarkan-four crew had clipped someone from the Serenity, the other big cargo ship currently in dock transferring shipments. The "disagreement" had turned into an all-out brawl right there in the loading bay. She'd never seen a fight with loading exos before, but they'd battered the hell out of each other in the middle of the deck.

Then, just as they'd gotten that sorted out, there had been a domestic on the westside habitation ring. It had resulted in a fatality, which had amounted to hours of paperwork, and her afternoon plans to catch up on admin had hightailed it over the horizon. She couldn't even bring herself to feel sorry for the guy whose corpse was rapidly cooling in the station morgue. His wife, one of the hull repair team, had caught him in bed with their neighbor. Given the wife was used to manhandling structural girders into place while out in deep space, the fact that she'd folded her cheating spouse into a human pretzel wasn't a surprise.

She sighed as she headed toward the lift to the station crew habitation levels. Thanks to the paperwork this afternoon, she had a shitload of work already lined up for tomorrow. Seriously, if anyone had told her how much paperwork there would be when she'd signed on as security chief for the station, she'd have run the other way. Fast.

"Hey, boss," a voice behind her called out. She turned to find Officer Mills behind her, a broad smile on his face. As the newest member of the security team, he'd made no pretense of his interest in her, asking her out at least once a week in the two months he'd been here. She didn't date. Not her staff, not anyone... not since her last lover had taken one look at the scars on her legs and shuddered. Oh, he'd quickly concealed the expression but not before she'd seen it. Now she could never *unsee* it.

So, even cute as Mills was, she'd knocked him back each time. It hadn't dimmed his enthusiasm. She steeled herself for the expected dinner or date invitation, dragging up one of her many prepared excuses to the tip of her tongue. But rather than ask her out, he indicated the sports bag over his shoulder.

"Just heading to the gym to work out. I wondered if you fancied sparring or something?"

Okay, that was a little better than a romantic dinner. He was cute—tall, blond and handsome with a winning smile—but she didn't date staff. That way led to issues with discipline and accusations of favoritism. But sparring... that wasn't a date. Any other time she might have been tempted, but she was exhausted. The bone-weariness that pulled at her frame reminded her that allowing one of her staff to hand her ass to her on a plate, or worse, just face-planting on the mats wasn't a good thing. It didn't inspire confidence.

"Some other time, Mills?" She smiled to soften the blow. "Long day and tomorrow's going to be even longer. Need to get some rack time."

His handsome face split into a wide grin. "I'll hold you to that! Night, boss. Sleep well."

She watched him for a moment as he walked down the corridor, whistling to himself happily. Shaking her head, she called the lift. She would never understand people like that, the ones who never seemed to let life get to them. One thing was for sure, she wanted some of whatever he was having.

The lift arrived, thankfully empty, and she stepped inside. Using her override as station security chief, she triggered the privacy setting so she could ride to her level in peace. Sure, it was an abuse of her power, but right now, she really didn't care. Leaning down, she finally gave in to the demands of her body and rubbed her leg just above the damaged knee joint.

She was only ten floors up, so the lift was there before she knew it. Stepping out, she trudged down the hall toward her quarters, keying in her code at the door. A cold chill washed over the back of her neck. She looked up sharply, sure someone was following her, but the corridor was empty.

Huh. She must be more tired than she'd thought. Shaking her head, she stepped inside and let the door slide shut behind her. Her personal quarters consisted of three tiny rooms: a bedroom, a bathroom, and a combined living and kitchen area. There wasn't enough room to swing a cat, not that she could afford something expensive like a pet. Fortunately, she didn't need much room, never had.

The pain in her leg ramped up to critical. She groaned as she flopped into the chair in front of the desk. Instead of the painkillers tucked into the top drawer, she reached for the bottle by the side of the console screen, pouring herself a generous measure.

The console beeped, indicating an incoming call. She groaned as she recognized the caller ID. Catherine Archer-Russell. Her mother. Great, just what she needed after the day she'd had. Punching the answer button, she plastered a wide smile on her face.

"Hi, Mom."

Her mother appeared on the screen, a neatly dressed woman in her mid-fifties although she would never admit to her actual age. Instantly her gaze cut to the glass in Eris's hand, and her scarlet lips pursed in disapproval.

"Eris... don't you think it's a little early for all that?"

Eris gritted her teeth and managed to keep the smile on her face. She'd been a disappointment to her social-climbing mother since the day she'd been medically discharged. *Especially* under the conditions she'd been discharged. The accident that had taken her out of active service had brought the company who'd manufactured the *Scorperio* units under investigation... The company her mother's husband part-owned.

Taking another swallow, she hissed under her breath as the whiskey burned all the way down to her stomach. It wouldn't deal with the pain, but at least it might allow her to fall asleep tonight.

"Why? The sun's over the yardarm. Somewhere. What do you want, Mom?"

Her mother settled back down, her outfit perfectly coordinated with the cream leather of her couch. "Can't I call my favorite daughter occasionally?"

"I'm your only daughter."

Catherine waved dismissively. "Have you heard from Eric?"

And there it was. She should have known her mom had only called for something to do with Eric. The golden child. Eris's twin brother and the shining star of the Archer family, he was a doctor of something or other—something so complicated Eris's eyes glazed over if she was ever forced to use his official title and area of specialty. Her mother liked to say he was the whole package—brains and looks to boot.

The problem was, he was an utter dick. And that wasn't even said with sibling affection. Eris wouldn't be in the same room as her twin if you paid her.

"Not recently, no," she deadpanned, taking another sip from her glass. And by recently, she meant in the last four years or so. "Probably got lost in research again. You know how he is."

"Oh yes," her mother trilled. "Of course. He's so busy, so many projects... he must be under so much pressure."

Eris tuned out, making inroads into her whiskey as she let her mother wax lyrical on her favorite subject until the glass was empty. Then she smiled.

"Great talk, Mom, but I have to go. Got an

incoming alert. A security chief's job is never done, you know!" she said, imitating Catherine's trill and making sure to add her official position in there. It always shut her mother up.

"Oh yes, of course, love. You know... I could talk to your father—"

"*Step*father."

"—talk to your father about getting you a position with the corporation closer to home."

Eris kept her gritted teeth behind her pleasant smile. Over her dead body. There was no way she'd go work for Max Russell even if her life depended on it. The guy was slime with a capital S. She always felt like she needed a month-long bath in bleach every time she spoke to the guy. She had no idea what her mother saw in him.

"I really think..."

"No need, Mom. I..." Sensing that her mother was working up to one of her tirades, Eris went for the one thing she knew would get her mother off her back for a while. "Well, there's a guy here and..."

"Oh!" Surprise and then delight filtered across her mother's surgery-enhanced features. "Why didn't you say so! I have been so looking forward to grandchildren! Who is h—"

"Gotta go, Mom. Needed on duty."

Eris cut the call and slumped back in her seat, running her hand through her hair. Then she groaned and looked at the whiskey bottle. First the doc and then her mom... bad luck always traveled in threes. What else did she have to look forward to?

2

*C*oming down here when she'd been drinking was never a good idea.

Eris walked down the corridor in the bowels of the station, heading for the storage units. This wasn't a civilian area, so she didn't have to worry about watching her back or some asshole trying to pick her pocket. Most of the light-fingered crowd on the station knew that trying to lift anything from her would result in broken fingers and a stay in the cells. Still, every so often a newbie would try something. Right now, she wasn't in the mood. Anyone who crossed her would likely end up with more than broken fingers. Much more.

She only passed one person on her way down to the units. Tucked behind the lowest of the docking bays, the corridor had a lovely view of the sweet fuck all that was space. For a moment, she paused by the window, looking out. The abyss called to her, the siren's call of nothingness to ease her wounded soul a temptation she knew to ignore.

Pushing off from the wall, she walked along the row of storage units. Each was marked with an alphanumeric painted on the door with a retinal scanner in the wall beside it.

She walked three-quarters of the way down the line and stopped in front of unit 74B-9. After staring the door down for a few moments, she triggered the scanner and picked the option for a retinal scan rather than an access code.

"Welcome, Chief Archer," the computer welcomed her as the door clamps released to swing open.

The lights snapped on as she stepped over the threshold, working their way down to the back. One of the larger units, it was big enough to contain a small land vehicle, but the hulking figure standing by the back wall wasn't anything so mundane.

Instead, it was one of the most dangerous weapons in earth history—an armored tank suit.

Her tank suit.

"Hey, old girl," Eris murmured in a low voice, walking toward it.

She ran a gentle hand down the arm, over the battered paint and metal. Her fingers traced the lettering on the breastplate.

Archer, E. Sgt. "Freya." AIU: 31

She'd found it in a surplus store a few months ago, in pieces and being sold for parts. After months of scouring the net for any mention of armored suits, she'd hardly dared to believe it. She'd expected it to be something else... part of an actual tank or a loading exoskeleton with plates welded to it being passed off as a *Scorperio*. As soon as she'd seen the shrouded shape, though, she'd known.

It was a shadow of its former self. When she'd found it, it had been little more than the torso cage and left leg. The arms and shoulder laser arrays were gone, but the left machine gun was still in place. It had been decommissioned, badly, but nothing an experienced suit operator/mechanic couldn't fix easily. Remarkably, the shielding was all still there, even for parts that were missing, and as far as she could work out from her brief suit-up, none of the power cells were corrupt.

She'd rebuilt it in here, sourcing the missing parts online. She hadn't been able to see something so glorious left to rack and ruin, even if she couldn't use it now. Not only could her body not take the neural load, but there were no mobile-tank units anymore. She had no idea what she was going to do with it when it was complete... donate it to a museum eventually, she guessed. But, for now, at times like these, she needed the comfort of an old friend.

Turning around, she slid to the floor with her back to one of the legs. Reaching in her pocket, she liberated her hip flask and unscrewed the top. She lifted it and toasted the hulking monolith behind her.

"Here's to us, old girl. We did our best but got left behind. Didn't we? At least we still got each other for the moment."

"Please tell me you've done this before," Zero said, eyeing the medical equipment as Talent set it up around him.

It looked a lot more complicated than anything he'd used on himself in the past. It was all wires and tubes as Talent connected the auto-diagnostic bed to the console on the other side of the room.

"Don't you need to have qualified as a healer to use all this?" he asked nervously, trying to slide off the bed without Talent spotting him. A sharp look from the tall Lathar pinned him in place.

"Not for these systems, no." Talent's hands moved confidently as he made sense of all the wires and plugged them in. "This is an auto-system so it doesn't need a neural link. Still, it's far in advance of the old scanners you guys were using. I can't believe you still had it boxed up in storage."

Zero shrugged. "None of us could make heads nor tails of it. You'd think they'd come with instructions or something."

"Well, that's what happens when you steal stuff." A smile curved Talent's lips as he knelt to put the last few connectors in place. "Yes, I'm well aware this unit was destined for the healer's hall on *Yxaniixos Seven.*"

Zero blinked. "How do you know that?" Even *he* hadn't known that, and he'd been the one to boost the container from its shipment.

"Auto-units aren't that common. When one goes missing, the healer's hall on Lathar Prime is informed. I was tasked with shipping a replacement unit out to them."

"Ahh."

That made sense. Medical units were expensive, but then again, so were imperial healers... and there was always the risk of falling out of favor with the empire and being barred, which was the reason they'd decided to "acquire" a unit. None of them had realized that simply setting one up required several decades of medical knowledge, a note from the lord healer, and a minor miracle.

"Okay... we should be good to go." Talent stood, slapping the side of the unit in satisfaction as he moved to stand behind the console. "Just lie as still as you can, no fidgeting. It'll help me get a good initial scan."

Zero grunted in reply and went still. With absolute control over his body, no one could go as still as a cyborg. Well, as still as him because as far as he knew... he was the only one of his kind in existence.

The machine whirred to life around him, intersecting holographic rings moving over and around each other as they scanned him. He didn't bother closing his eyes. He just focused inward and let his onboard inform him about what was going on.

He could tell he was being scanned, right down to the molecular level and... it itched. Ignoring the irritation, he pondered the feeling. His own systems were a constant source of fascination for him. Even though he had no memories before the point T'Raal had pulled him half-dead from the wreckage of his ship, he knew several things about himself.

He had been made. Not born.

There was no other explanation for it. Analysis of his skeletal structure and the enhancements made to it indicated that his implants were approximately six months younger than his biological components. Which meant either he'd come out of the womb an adult, or... yeah, he hadn't been born.

He'd been grown somehow.

The tickle from the scanning ramped up a notch as the machine began a low-level whine of complaint. Too low for an unenhanced being to detect, the machine seemed to work harder to scan him. Probably because he was mostly machine.

Given that, was he even a person?

Yes. He was. He had to believe that. He was capable of independent thought, even when he shut his onboard down as far as he dared, to the bare minimum required to run his cybernetics. He was alive... and sentient... but past that, he didn't know anything about himself. Even the few serial codes he could dig up from his base coding weren't a match for anything from any known world or civilization.

Not even humanity, the latest species to join the intergalactic community.

Still, he couldn't help a little curiosity over what Talent, formerly a member of the healer's hall on Lathar Prime, would discover. The tickle in his body ramped up again. He gritted his teeth when it became an unpleasant buzz. Hopefully, this would be over soon.

"Interesting." Tal's voice was low. "Physically, your biological construction mirrors the Lathar. Same bodily systems from what I can see. Your skeletal structure has been enhanced with an alloy I don't recognize, and most of your joints are cybernetic. Internal organs are protected with mesh, again that I don't recognize but your brain and ner... what the *draanth?*"

The whine of complaint from the unit became a scream, and the intersecting rings circling him went into a frenzy.

"*Trall!*" Talent hissed, hands moving frantically over the console. "It's overloading. I can't shut it down!"

Zero heard the explosion before it started, that moment of stillness before a spark caught and fire flared.

"*Out! Now!*"

Talent moved faster than anyone Zero had ever seen before, shoving the big cyborg out the door ahead of him and slamming his hand over the door release. He heard a roar like all the hounds of hell had been released behind them in their fiery rage and then silence as the door slid shut behind them.

BOOOOOM!

Both men winced as the explosion hit, almost buckling the door of the medbay. Talent opened his mouth to speak, but Zero shook his head, pointing upward.

Sure enough, within a half-second, T'Raal's voice exploded over the comm. *"What the fuck have you lot done to my ship?"*

Less than ten seconds later, the heavily muscled Lathar barreled down the corridor toward them followed by the rest of the crew. T'Raal skidded to a halt, his hands on his hips as he looked at the pair of them.

His eyes narrowed as he spotted the door and then he rounded on Talent.

"Okay, *him* I understand... give him half a chance, and something gets blown up. But you? And *medbay?*"

"'Snot his fault, boss," Zero argued and stood

upright. He shook his head to try and clear the ringing. "He was scanning me and... well, boom!"

"Boom?" T'Raal didn't look convinced, glancing over at Talent.

"Boom." Talent nodded in agreement. "Never seen a unit react that way before. I was just starting to scan your power core and..."

"Boom?" Fin, leaning one shoulder against the wall, asked.

"Yes! Exactly! Boom!" the medic agreed, his face alight with fascination. "We need to find another unit and scan again—"

T'Raal squeaked, cutting him off. "Not on the *Sprite*, you're not! Fuck's sake, is there even anything left of medbay?"

Zero winced and moved toward the door. Tentatively, he put his hand on the metal. It was buckled but not hot. Reaching out, he uplinked with the *Sprite*'s systems.

"Sensors are toast in there," he reported. "But hull integrity is uncompromised. It looks like the room contained the blast."

"Lucky for you," T'Raal grunted, but Zero had caught his quick looks of concern when he'd arrived, making sure neither of them was injured. "You two are on cleanup duty. We'll need to divert for resupply."

Zero's heart leaped. Resupply meant they were headed where Lathar feared to tread, to the outer limits of Terran space. Unlike the Latharian empire and other powers, independents like the Warborne had known about the human species for a while. They only ever ventured along the edges of human territory, making sure to only visit the most outlying stations and colonies.

But one of those was Tarantus Station. And that meant the beautiful station security chief, Eris Archer.

Eris was so not a morning person.

She grunted as she sat down on the bed slowly and ran a hand through her loose hair. Reaching for her brace, she avoided looking at her leg. Scars made a patchwork of her skin, telling the tale of her shattered limb and highlighting the sites of her implants. The scars were smooth, old and silvery. No one would guess the damn things were burning out.

With a sigh, she buckled the exoskeleton in place, making sure the contact points on the brace were sited correctly over the implant points that powered it. In an instant, the heaviness of the limb disappeared, and she stood easily. Quickly she pulled her uniform pants on, covering the brace. Unless the fabric was pulled tightly, no one would even know it was there.

She braided her hair as she walked out of the door, uniform neat and in place, heading for the lift. A quick stop at one of the central promenade retailers on the way to her office snagged her a coffee and a pastry, and she whistled to herself as she walked through the door.

"Hey, beautiful," a familiar voice made her freeze and then groan internally. One of the night shift officers had Jayce Allen in cuffs leaning up against the booking desk. The cells were arranged along the walls of the central area, which could be used as a holding cell itself in case of more significant incidents.

Allen grinned and winked at her. "Miss me?"

"Like a hole in the head," she growled as she approached the desk, holding her hand out for the booking sheet. Her thigh pocket gave a buzz, indicating an incoming message on her personal display flex, but she ignored it for the moment. If it was anything important, the computer would let her know.

"See?" Sparky rolled his head on his shoulder to

grin at the booking officer Mills. "Told ya she loves me."

"Really." For once Mills was unamused, shooting Sparky a glare.

"Can you confirm your name?"

Allen grinned. "Your gorgeous boss knows who I am."

Eris read through the report. Public disorder offenses. *Again.* "He needs you to confirm your name. Legal reasons."

He leaned back against the counter, propped on his elbows. "Sparky."

She sighed and handed the sheet back to Mills. "Full name, not a nickname, or we'll put you in the system as a John Doe, and it'll be a forty-eight not a twelve-hour hold."

Rolling his eyes at her, Allen turned around and leaned on the counter. "Jayce Theodore Allen."

"Theodore?"

"Yeah, I'm a teddy bear. Wanna give me a cuddle?"

Mills slapped the form down on the counter, almost taking Sparky's nose off. "Sign here."

"Can't write, squire. Will a thumbprint do?"

"Ignore him, Mills," Eris said, heading toward

her office. "He reads and writes seven languages, including assholian. Don't take any of his crap."

"Hey! I resemble that remark!"

She shook her head and shut her office door, cutting off Sparky's protests. She watched as the tall guy straightened up and signed the form before Mills escorted him toward a cell opposite her office. Great, she got to look at the wise-cracking asshole all day.

But rather than gesticulate to her all day, the lanky blond settled down, stretching full length on the narrow bunk and covering his eyes with his arm. Why was he back? The last time she'd seen him he was leaving with a new crew, none of whom she'd been able to find in the station database or in any police records anywhere.

Her eyes narrowed as she pulled up the logs again and checked her searches. Given the dark rings tattooed around Allen's upper arms, she'd even called in a few favors and checked a highly illegal copy of the Mirax Corp's records. She needed to know if she had a potential problem on her hands. But... nothing, zip, nada.

In fact, nothing came up on *any* of the searches she'd run, even after extending them out to the entire Terran systems network. None of the three men Allen had left with existed *anywhere,* on any system.

"Impossible."

She pulled the footage up again, studying the three men. They were, in a word, massive and heavily muscled. One had long hair and an almost pirate-like swagger while the other two were short-haired. One, the guy who'd spoken to Allen, was intense and focused... and all of them had a dangerous aura, but the final man, with the short hair and the gloves, drew her attention the most.

She leaned forward, studying the screen intensely. Not much footage of the three was available, only what she'd been able to recover from the promenade security feeds and some from the side corridors. All of it showed Allen chatting away to his friends, the group's body language easy and relaxed as they walked. But the feeds cut out when they headed down to the docks. She knew they'd been on dock eight, but once again, the feeds down there were on the fritz, and she had no footage from that time period.

"Dammit!" she hissed, slamming her hands against the edge of her desk as the screen stilled on a freeze-frame. Her mystery man had chosen just that moment to look over his shoulder and up at the camera. She could almost believe the smile on his lips was for her, that he knew she was watching, but that was ridiculous.

Leaning forward, she frowned. "Who the hell are you?"

3

*T*arantus Station was the same battered, shitty little outpost he remembered. Zero smiled as they dropped out of high speed a short way off the station, and it came into view. His hands, metal and organic, moved over the console with ease and confidence as he zoomed the view on the central screen to a close-up of the station. Light from a nearby star glinted off the metal, peeled paint, and rust patches telling the tale of maintenance left to the ravages of insufficient budgets and mismanagement. He was surprised some areas were even still habitable.

Concern filled him as his gaze scanned over the bulbous central core, with its habitation rings rising like arms from the main body. Where did Eris live?

Was she in danger if an airlock gave or a bulkhead blew? His muscles locked up as he fought the need to gun the engines and get to her as quickly as possible. The sheer force of the need shook him. He'd never had such a response to a woman before.

"Any word from Sparky yet?" he asked over his shoulder as he smoothly dropped them onto the approach vector station control had allocated them. They were known here, so their transponder signal and arrival hadn't caused any alarm. A lot of that was down to the *Sprite's* chameleon systems.

Holographic emitter arrays dotted the hull and altered the appearance of the ship to that of a human trader vessel. They'd have to get up close and personal, close enough to touch the hull, to figure out what they were seeing was false. As another precaution, he made sure to uplink with the base as they docked and knocked out the security cameras on the docking arm as well. In a place like Tarantus, with its strained maintenance schedule, no one thought twice about it.

"Nope, nothing," Skinny, their comms officer, replied. "No response at all."

"That's not like him." Zero frowned as he cycled down the engines and levered himself out of the pilot's chair. Beauty was ready and waiting to take his place, his eyes gleaming with anticipation of finally getting to fly Zero's baby.

He shot out a hand, gripping the smaller man by the shoulder. "Not even a *scratch*. Understand?" he demanded in a warning growl. "No bumps, no scrapes... I don't want to hear so much as a bolt rattle on her when you get back. Okay?"

"You got it, big man." Beauty smiled. It was meant to be reassuring, but... yeah, Zero *knew* Beauty. The guy might be one of the quietest members of the Warborne, keeping to himself a lot of the time, but Zero had seen him in combat. He was utterly bat-shit crazy, and that gleam in his eye said he was a speed demon.

"Still don't like it."

T'Raal, sitting in the captain's chair in the middle of the bridge, grunted. "Your call. We need supplies from Praxis-Four, so fly us there yourself or let Beauty fly so you can go 'find' Sparky."

His mocking air quotes were accompanied by a small smirk that made Zero groan mentally. T'Raal hadn't been fooled by his concern for the human ex-con after all.

"Yeah, yeah... I'm going," he grumbled, grabbing his pack and slinging it over one broad shoulder.

The *Sprite* was so small he was out of the airlock

and walking down the docking arm corridor within minutes. Behind him, he heard the airlock shut and start to cycle as Beauty prepared the ship to leave. His hackles rose for a second, but he forced the feeling down. He was on his own here, yes, but he was more than capable of taking care of himself. And he had an ally on station... if he could find whichever hole the wily smart-mouthed human had disappeared down.

Heading for the central area, he made his way up to the upper promenade levels. Several people watched him with interest as he passed, so he made sure they got a good look at the heavy energy-pistols holstered on his hips. That usually discouraged even the nosiest among them. He suppressed his snigger as they all abruptly found something other than him way more interesting. Like the floor. Or the ceiling.

The upper level contained most of the bars on the stations, so it was empty this time of day. From what he knew of Sparky, that would make absolutely no difference. He seemed to be equal opportunities when it came to sex and alcohol.

Wandering into the bar he knew Sparky frequented, he paused for a moment as if to allow his vision to adjust to the darker interior. He didn't need it, but squinting was a useful cover for him to scan the interior of the bar.

His grin widened. Sparky wasn't in here, but his search wasn't a total bust. There, over the other side of the bar, her back to him, was Eris Archer.

Four hours of dealing with paperwork was more than enough hell for one woman, so by dinner time, Eris was ready to scream. To add insult to injury, the message that had been waiting for her on her personal flex was from her brother. Sighing, she'd ignored it. The third bit of bad luck. The last thing she needed was her asshole twin guilt-tripping her over whatever bee their mother had in her bonnet now.

So she'd escaped to Pat's bar for her version of "me time." She always sat at the rear of the bar with her back to the room. It stopped people talking to her and interrupting her little oasis of calm in the middle of the day.

Sighing, she lifted her coffee and closed her eyes, breathing in the steam from the top of the mug. She took a sip and murmured in pleasure. The stuff in the office was okay. It was hot and wet, but that was all that could be said about it. The coffee in Pat's was the proper filter stuff and a balm to her soul. She treated herself to a couple more sips before she turned her attention to the toasted sandwich on her plate.

She was halfway through it when she became aware of someone's attention. Her gaze flicked up to the mirror on the back wall to see someone weaving his way through the tables toward her. Not just any someone, but the same man she'd been studying earlier this morning on her security screens.

Allen's mysterious friend.

She blinked and pinched herself, in case she'd fallen asleep in her office and this was all a dream. But nope, other than a sharp pain in her thigh, nothing altered. Tall, dark and handsome still walked toward her... and she still had a mouthful of sandwich.

"Hey," he smiled as he reached her table, the dimples in his cheeks as sexy as all hell. "Do you mind if I join you?"

She raised an eyebrow as she swallowed quickly. There were empty tables all around them and men like this? They usually didn't come on to women like her. She was too tall, too slender and too acerbic for anyone to want to flirt with. Eric had always been the charismatic one, not her.

"Why?"

She groaned to herself as the comment slipped out. Blunt and to the point, it was just this side of confrontational.

But he didn't seem perturbed. Instead, he grabbed a chair, turned it around, and sat straddled, his heavily muscled arms folded over the back. "Because you're the most beautiful woman I've ever seen."

She just looked at him. The silence stretched out. Then she laughed.

"Yeah... right?" She looked around them quickly. "Okay, so where are they?"

He frowned. "Who?"

"The camera crew that leaps out to say 'surprise!'" She picked up her coffee again and took a sip. "I take a dim view of shit like that. And believe me, pissing off the head of security on a place like this isn't a place you wanna be."

His expression froze, and he looked at her curiously. "You think this is a joke? Why?"

She snorted, putting her cup down with a small click. "Men like you do not look twice at women like me," she told him shortly, really in no mood for crap like this today.

Yeah, sure, she might have semi-obsessed over him on the security feeds, but that was it. The charm offensive had to have an ulterior motive. Like Grayson, her shuddering ex, who had wined and dined her to get an in with station security so he could ship his hinky shipments without issues. Fortunately, she'd seen his game early on and thrown him in the cells herself. "So either your buddies have put you up to it, or you want something."

"Someone hurt you, badly. Didn't they?" he mused, rubbing at the stubble on his oh-so-kissable jaw with strong fingers.

"Pop-psychology as well, huh?" She was on the defensive now, her back well up. "What's with the one-glove look? Some off-world fashion someplace?"

His eyebrow winged up a little, and she caught a flash of anger in his eyes, quickly smothered. Ha... so Mister Charm wasn't as unrufflable as he seemed. Was he?

Pushing upright, he pulled the black leather glove off his hand, yanking at the fingers before sliding it off. The glove hit the table. Her mouth opened and closed like a guppy as heat spread over her cheeks. Metal met her gaze. His right hand was a replacement.

"I do apologize. I didn't realize you were..."

His lips quirked. "What? Devastatingly handsome? Charming in wit? Intelligent?"

"Differently abled," she ground out, more annoyed with herself than him. She'd taken the mickey out of his glove when he was hiding his replacement hand and that had been cruel. "I apologize. I shouldn't have made fun of your glove."

He reached out and covered her hand with his, the organic one. "Hey... it's okay," he murmured, obviously sensing her distress. "Really. I'm not sensitive about it. And I'm not just differently abled, beautiful... I'm differently *gifted.*"

She couldn't help the small snort that escaped her. "Gifted, huh?"

"You'd better believe it, baby."

"Obviously humility didn't come as part of the package."

He grinned. "No need, not with my package. But you know what they say..."

She'd been about to clap him back for the package comment but lifted an eyebrow. "No, what do they say?"

"The proof of the pudding's in the eating," he drawled. "So how about it, beaut? Take a chance on me?"

She recovered her hand, instantly missing the

warmth of his touch. Leaning back in her chair, she looked at him over the rim of her cup. "You? I thought we were talking about your package?"

His eyes darkened. "You can take that out for a spin any time you like, sweetheart. I just thought you'd like to be wined and dined first..."

"And we're right back to why. And don't give me that crap about me being the most beautiful woman you've ever seen... unless you need optical implants as well."

He just winked at her and tapped his left temple. "Who says I didn't?"

Oh god... she wanted the ground to open and swallow her whole. Just one problem with that. No ground on a station and she'd seen the maintenance sublevels. No way did she want to end up down there. She'd probably end up with an infection or a nasty skin rash.

She finished her coffee and put the cup back down, pushing it away. "Well... it was nice talking to you, Mr...?"

"Zero." He smiled.

"Mr. Zero," she corrected herself as she stood. "But I'm afraid I need to get back to work."

"It's just Zero." He stood at the same time. "What time do you get off work?"

"I'm afraid I'm pulling the graveyard tonight," she said with a smile, totally brushing him off. She had a name now, so she could find out more about him. Even if she had to impound his damn ship to find out who the hell he and his friends were. "Perhaps see you around."

And with that, she left quickly.

Her quip to Zero had been meant as a brush off, but less than four hours later it turned out to be unwittingly prophetic.

"You have to be kidding me?" she asked, her expression flat and totally unimpressed. "You're telling me they BOTH managed to get themselves a medbay trip?"

Mills looked uncomfortable, shifting his weight from foot to foot. "I'm afraid so, boss," he grimaced. "Ward called out a warning, but Nelson didn't hear him and piled through the door right after him. They both got hit as the door shorted out."

She groaned, closing her eyes. Yeah, she knew some of her staff weren't the brightest bulbs in the box since places like Tarantus didn't attract the cream of the crop, but come on... was common sense too much to ask for?

"Right, okay," she sighed, opening her eyes. "Is tonight the only shift that needs covering?"

"Uh-huh." Mills handed her the staffing sheet. "I managed to move everyone else around. We'll be a little short for a few days until Baires gets back from leave but we can manage."

She gave a small smile. "Whatever would I do without you, Mills?"

He opened his mouth, a gleam of hope in his eyes. She slapped the staffing sheet into the middle of his chest. "And no, that doesn't mean dinner... or anything else. I don't date my staff."

His face fell a little, but then he grinned. "Can't blame a guy for trying. Can you?"

She chuckled as she stole his new coffee, still steaming in its plasti-mug. "Nope. Now get your ass out of here before I change my mind and make you pull a double shift."

He was headed to the door almost before she'd finished the sentence. "Thanks, boss. See you tomorrow!"

Cradling her purloined drink, she settled herself behind the desk. When she looked up, she caught Allen grinning at her from his cell. "What are you grinning at?"

He was sitting up, leaning against the wall with

one forearm against a raised knee. "The foolishness of youth. That kid never had a chance with you, but fair play to him for trying."

Her hackles rose a little. "How do you know he didn't have a chance?"

Allen's lips quirked. "He's a kid. You'd eat him for breakfast."

"Oh, so I'm a maneater now. Am I?"

Before Allen could reply, the double doors slid open and Mills walked back through, face like thunder as he pushed a cuffed man ahead of him.

Zero.

She was out of her seat before she knew it and halfway across the space between them. Mills was sporting a livid bruise around one eye.

"What the hell happened?"

"This asshole," Mills snarled, shoving Zero forward and slapping a gun-belt with some heavy-duty hardware in it on the booking desk. Zero's weaponry. He'd been wearing it buckled around his hips in the bar earlier. "Decided to just randomly clock me as soon as I walked out the door. No idea why. Just walked up to me and *wham!* Almost landed me on my ass!"

Eris raised an eyebrow. "Left or right hook?"

"Right. Why?"

"Uh-huh, no reason." She motioned Zero forward. "I'll book him. Don't worry. Go get that seen to. Okay?"

Mills stood for a moment, anger written in every line of his frame. Then he nodded. "You sure you don't need me here, boss? He's dangerous."

"I'll be fine. Don't worry. I'll arm the auto-defenses if necessary."

He didn't look convinced, but she shooed him toward the door anyway. "Head to medical and get that checked out. You could have cracked your orbital socket or have a concussion or something."

"I'm sure I'll be fine. I think I should st—"

"*Go!*" she ordered, pointing at the door while grabbing Zero by the arm. The sound of the door opening and closing behind them told her the officer had left.

"Alone at last," Zero's lips quirked as he looked down at her. Gods above, he was tall... and broad.

"Is that why you decked my officer?" she demanded. "To get me alone in here? And don't think I don't realize what you did..." She grabbed his right arm, the metal hard under her fingers. "If you'd wanted to hurt him, you would have. So you didn't want to hurt him... Well, I have news for you. Your plan failed."

"Oh?" He leaned in. The scent of his cologne, warmed by his skin, made her weak at the knees. "I dunno. I think it worked pretty well."

"Apart from the fact we're not alone." She leaned around him and nodded toward Allen.

Zero turned and nodded. "Hey, Sparky. How's it hanging?"

The ex-con grinned. "Oh, you know, to the left as usual."

She almost groaned. They knew each other. Of course they knew each other.

"Since you two are on such good terms, I'll stick you in together. You can keep each other company."

Allen unfolded himself from the bunk and sauntered toward the energy field at the front. "Yeah... sorry, doll, but I do believe my time is up."

"Of course it is."

There weren't enough curse words in existence to adequately express her frustration at the current situation. All she could do was go with it.

"Computer, release prisoner Allen, J."

"Yes, Chief Archer," the security computer replied, its feminine voice all sex worker breathiness. It had grated on her nerves since she'd arrived but never more so than today. She'd get it recoded tomorrow. First thing.

"Later, 'gators!" Allen quipped as he sauntered out of the cell when the forcefield snapped off. "Don't do anything I wouldn't do."

Winking at them, he disappeared through the main doors.

"Seems to know his way around," Zero commented.

"You could say he's a regular guest. In," she ordered, nodding toward the cell.

He inclined his head and stepped into the cell. Sensing an occupant without a security identity tag, the forcefield snapped back on, throwing up a shimmering blue wall between them. At the same moment, the nano-bonds on his plasti-cuffs gave, dropping to the floor in little more than dust.

"Would you like to tell me why you wanted to get locked up?" she asked, sliding her flexi out of her thigh pocket to book him in.

"What makes you say that?"

He stood in the middle of the cell, studying his surroundings. They weren't much—three bare walls, the fourth made up of the barrier between them, and one bunk bolted to the wall. The facilities were the same, bolted to the wall behind a half-height privacy screen. Somehow though, despite the fact he and Allen were of a similar height, he managed to make the cell seem tiny.

"You only gave officer Mills a black eye," she said, nodding toward his metal arm. "Yet if you'd wanted to, you could have put his head through a bulkhead. So... you hit him, but not hard. Just hard enough to get arrested. Why?"

He turned and sat on the narrow bunk recently vacated by Allen.

"I would have thought that was obvious," he looked at her meaningfully.

She barked a laugh in surprise. "You really don't take rejection well. Do you?"

Looking up, an undignified squeak escaped her, and she almost dropped her pad. He was right on the other side of the barrier, looking at her intently. She hadn't heard him move, nor had she ever seen anyone move that quickly or silently before.

"Name?" Her voice was sharp as she tried to cover the fact that he'd startled her. Well, ignore it anyway and if he had any instinct of self-preservation, he would totally let her and not say a thing.

"I told you... Zero."

Her fingers paused over the screen. "That's not a name. It's a number."

He folded massive arms over his equally massive chest. "It's the only one I got, beautiful."

"Alright." She shrugged and entered the single name into the system.

"World of origin?"

"Unknown."

She looked up. "What do you mean 'unknown'?"

"Exactly that." His smile wasn't as cocky as before. "I have no idea what planet I'm from."

He reached up with his metal hand and tapped the side of his temple gently. "Long-term memory before I woke up like this..." He waggled his fingers. "All gone."

Shit. He must have lost his memory in the accident that had given him the replacement.

"No worries. Current planet of residence?"

"Lathar Prime."

And just like that, all her guilt at quizzing him disappeared, anger taking its place.

"Oh, for fuck's sake. Will you take this seriously?" she demanded.

Lathar Prime.

She'd heard of the Lathar, of course. Who hadn't? Like the rest of the human population across the territories, she'd been glued to the newsfeeds. But... he didn't look anything like the leather-clad alien barbarians. "You do realize I can charge you with obstruction of a security officer's duties?"

He arched an eyebrow. "Does that mean I get you cuffing me this time, Officer? Because if so, I'm all in."

"It's *Chief!*" she hissed, turning as the department doors swished open. The interruption was timely and would stop her from committing murder in her own department.

Her brows snapped together as a guy wearing the uniform of Michael's, the premier and only restaurant on the station, wheeled a delivery trolley in.

"Errr... can I help you?" she asked, forcing her voice to its polite setting.

"Yeah, I got an ultimate romance dinner delivery for a..." The delivery guy checked his list. "For a Mister Naught?"

"*Zero?*" They both chorused at once, and he grinned.

"Yeah, that's it. Where do you want it?"

4

"*I* know where I'd like to put it," Eris ground out, voice clipped.

She waved the poor delivery guy to leave the trolley by the booking desk and turned on Zero. For a woman he was trying his utmost to charm, the amount of fury in her eyes made him take a physical step back.

"So, this was all a setup, huh?" Her voice was quiet.

Hope filled him, and he tilted his head to the side slightly. "More 'creating an opportunity'?"

She nodded and he took a step forward. Perhaps she was just annoyed they'd been interrupted? Sure, he was on the wrong side of a security barrier for what he really wanted... to pull her into his arms and see if her lips were as soft as they looked... but that was better than her initial reaction.

His onboard tickled at the back of his mind, trying to get his attention. He ignored it, far more interested in the woman in front of him.

"So... what happens now?" She tilted her head to look up at him. This close, he was struck by how much smaller than him she was. That was to be expected, though. He was a large male, bigger physically than most males of any species. Even if she was tall for a human... they were one of the smallest species in the galaxy.

It was also a leading question, and he knew he was being tested. Nothing about her body language and demeanor said as much. Still, women were women, no matter what the species, and the look in her eyes told him to tread carefully.

"Well..." he drawled, leaning one shoulder against the wall nearest to him. "I was kind of hoping you'd drop this barrier, and we could have a nice, romantic meal."

His onboard flagged him again, the interruption getting more insistent. Not wanting to divert his attention, he suppressed the notification.

"Really now?" her voice was sickly sweet, and she smiled.

Shit. That was so not a good smile.

The notification tickled again. This time his onboard didn't give him a choice. It broke through his suppression, flaring a warning across his vision.

Incoming hostiles detected. Take evasive action.

The smile fled from his face, and he straightened up.

"Eris, you need to let me out of this cell. Right now," he ordered, focusing on the door. His onboard had been idly monitoring the security feeds on the station, and it had picked up coordinated movement coming their way.

She chuckled, starting to turn away. "Yeah, right. Like I'm going to do that. Pro tip... if you want to impress a woman, don't get arrested. But... thank you for the food, I'm sure the lads will appreciate it in the morning."

"Seriously, Eris, you're in danger!" he exclaimed, using his uplink to the station to monitor the corridor outside security. Armed men in black masks flooded into the area, any civilians fleeing quickly. No heroism or warning in a place like this.

Hostiles approaching active zone. Prepare to engage.

"Yeah, yeah..." She walked away from him toward the front of the booking desk. Where she was, she'd be directly in the firing line when those assholes came through the door.

"Bollocks."

He hadn't wanted to do this. Closing his eyes, Zero diverted all his processing power for a second to break into the security department system. Monitoring the primary station feeds was one thing, but the security department was a separate, more sophisticated system. It took him over a second to crack, an unforgivable delay before the forcefield snapped off.

"What th—?"

Eris didn't finish her sentence before he had her, forcing her down behind the booking desk as the front doors shattered. He curled his larger body around hers as the air around them was peppered with gunfire. The delivery trolley was the first to buy it. Bullets ripped through the thin metal and sent the chicken chasseur dancing in the air like a prima ballerina.

She didn't scream but instantly went for her gun, the weapon in her hand as she edged toward the corner of the desk, ready to return fire. He helped by plunging the department into darkness while reaching up to grab his gun belt. But it skittered from his fingers, dropping out of reach on the other side.

"Bollocks." Okay, he was going into this unarmed. It wasn't anything he hadn't done before and he was hardier than most.

"Shit," she hissed, ducking around the edge of the desk and firing off a couple of bursts. Two dull thuds followed... bodies hitting the floor. "Two down... six to go."

Her voice was low but he still heard her over the clatter of gunfire. Catching her gaze, he pointed to himself and indicated to the left. For a split second her eyes filled with confusion but then she nodded. Holding three fingers up, he counted down. On zero, they both broke from cover, Eris firing with a precision that warmed his combat-bitten heart. His girl was awesome, dropping her targets like a machine.

He roared as he broke cover, drawing the attention of the black-clad soldiers in the room. It was easy to see from the way they moved they were experienced in combat. Deadly.

He was deadlier.

The first guy swung around, bringing his rifle to bear. Zero grabbed the muzzle, shoving it upward even as the soldier fired. The bullets disturbed the air by his ear before ripping through the ceiling tiles above them. A lighting unit was hit and showered them with sparks.

Zero snarled as he slammed a hand into the guy's throat, crushing his windpipe. A second later, he'd flipped the gun out of his opponent's hands and fired. Using all his senses, both organic and cybernetic, he stepped over his fallen opponent and turned the rifle on the others. Bullets spat. One managed to tag him, his onboard registering the hits but instantly suppressing his pain reaction. Two shots later and only he and Eris were left standing.

He looked at her. She stood over the bodies she'd just gunned down of the men who'd tried to kill her, hair wild and her chest heaving. Their gazes clashed and held.

"We need to get out of here," he told her, his onboard warning him of more movement heading their way. Bending down, he scooped up his gun belt and buckled it on. "Or we're sitting ducks."

She had no choice but to trust him.

Eris checked her ammunition and nodded, gesturing toward the door. She'd have time to figure out what was going on when they were free and clear. For a second, he looked like he wanted to say something but then just turned toward the door, recovering a weapon from one of the fallen bodies before they moved out into the corridor.

Not allowing herself to look down at the corpses, she followed him. They moved automatically as a team, covering each other and firing arcs as though they'd been operating in combat together for years. Even though she was years removed from live combat situations and wasn't in her armored suit, she fell right back into old habits. It was like sliding into a comfortable pair of slippers.

Her leg ached, but she ignored it in favor of focusing on her surroundings as they moved through the corridors. She had no idea where they were going, but it really didn't matter. Anywhere away from the security department and the central area was good. The first because they could easily be bottle-necked and trapped there and the second because any shoot-out would cause massive loss of civilian life. As station security chief, she wanted to avoid that at all costs... even if people were trying to kill her.

She wouldn't have civilians in danger, not on her watch.

The corridors were mostly deserted. Like rats, the station occupants had a sixth sense when shit was going down and had fled the main areas. The few people they encountered ran as soon as they spotted the pair, hightailing it down corridors or through doors before she could warn them to get out of the public areas.

The emergency lighting had come on, rendering the corridors dark with low-level light. Better for them, but she couldn't help the shiver that stole along her spine. The atmosphere had turned the station from the semi-friendly place she knew to something ominous and foreboding, harboring potential enemies around each corner.

"If we head down to the storage bays," she said in a low voice, moving past Zero as he covered the corridor, "there's a small unused office down there and we can access the security logs from there. Find out what the fuck is going on."

She took up the next position and he replied when he moved past her. "Clear space coming up ahead. We'll need to cross it then drop down a level."

She nodded in assent, knowing the section he meant. One of the larger lounges, it was occasionally used as an arrivals lounge. In other words, it was a large area they needed to cross without any cover available.

Her heart thundered in her ears as they reached

the end of the corridor and stepped out into the clear. Regulating her breathing, she kept in step with Zero, noting he'd shortened his stride to match hers. Approval filled her. He wasn't at all the hoo-rah and gung-ho type she'd assumed.

He was definitely a soldier, though. Her gaze flicked to the hand cannons he carried like they were nothing. They weren't a design she recognized. Perhaps something experimental... which raised the question as to who the fuck he was? A spec ops soldier undercover? That would account for the fantastical story he'd given her about being from Lathar Prime. As if she'd fall for crap like that.

Halfway across the hall, the automated screens flicked from the usual colonization ads.

"Breaking news..." Red banners screamed across the screens, followed by an image of her face. "An alert has gone out for Terran First Terrorist Eris Archer. Archer... accused of the mass murder of civilians during the Krath-Seven campaign... has recently been sighted in the Tarantus system, where it is believed she was posing as security personnel."

She almost stopped dead, the blood draining from her face. "What the fuck? I was never anywhere near Krath-Seven."

Zero shoulder-bumped her to keep her moving.

"Answers the question as to who they're after," he rumbled in a deep voice as he covered their rear. "Someone's gone to a shit-load of trouble to frame you. Any idea why?"

"Not a clue," she growled, ignoring the screens as they blared about the price on her head. "But that's a fucking fortune. Every bounty hunter on the base will be out looking for me."

"Yeah... kinda think that's the point."

Zero's face was grim as they reached the corridor on the other side of the hall. She felt the presence of that ticking clock like a sword hanging over her head.

They were both silent as they moved through the corridors. Down here, the "luxury" smooth paneling of the main areas gave way to bare metal. She made sure to roll her feet as she placed them to avoid her boots clanging on the decking. Zero moved just as soundlessly, taking point as she covered the rear.

Suddenly he lifted a hand, his fist bunched. She froze in place, waiting for orders.

"We've got company, ahead and to the right," he murmured, his voice pitched low so it didn't carry. "Can't back up. Won't make it before they're on us."

Before he'd finished speaking, he turned and grabbed her around the waist. In a move worthy of a ballroom dancer, he whirled her through a door that appeared in the smooth metal of the wall.

Her eyes widened as she got a glimpse of an automated maintenance closet in the split second before the door closed behind them, plunging them into darkness. How the hell had he even known this was here, never mind managed to get it open? They were only used by cleaning bots, no one else should have access.

"Shit, scans said they were down this corridor..." a voice reached them through the thin metal of the door.

"Fucking tin can. They should've shot her when those fucking units were decommissioned. Unstable motherfuckers."

She winced at the conversation as the men looking for them paused on the other side of the door. Armored units had not been popular. A lot of vets blamed them for being discharged and sent home. She'd never understood why they couldn't see the mobile units hadn't taken their jobs but had saved lives. A tank suit was more durable, faster, and just plain harder to kill than a regular soldier. But a lot hadn't seen it that way and had celebrated when the truth came out that the mobile suits nearly always killed or crippled their operators in the end.

"Must've doubled back. Let's check the next intersection."

The sound of booted feet running echoed through the door and then silence only punctuated by the sound of their breathing. She looked up, Zero finally coming into view in the dimness of the closet. There was just enough light from the cleaning bots stacked in their charging pods around them for her to see him.

Then she realized she was pressed up close and personal against a solidly muscled, very male body. Even the bits of him that weren't metal might as well be; he was that solidly built.

"Fuck, what do they feed you? Solid titanium?" she whispered, trying to put some distance between them. However, the smallness of the closet put an end to that. As soon as she moved back, the bots behind her cheeped softly in protest. Her eyes widened. Their proximity alarms would reveal their hiding place to anyone in the corridor beyond.

His arm tightened around her waist, and she realized it was metal as well, not just the hand. But he didn't hurt her, pulling her in just tightly enough so she nestled against his broad chest. Lifting his other hand, he brushed the hair back from her cheek.

"Something like that... but I have a fondness for strawberries and cream," he whispered back, his voice a rough rumble in the darkness that sent a shiver along her skin like an auditory caress. "And my mind tells me that's exactly what you'll taste like when I kiss you."

"Really? And who says you're going to find out whether I do or not?"

Her hands spread out over the top of his chest, fingertips flirting with the line of his collarbones under his shirt. One found the edge where flesh met metal, and she flinched a little, not expecting it. But a few seconds later she replaced her hands. She shouldn't, but she couldn't help herself. Everything about him was fascinating. It shouldn't be. Not when she had a bounty on her head and people out to kill her.

His thumb brushed against her cheek. She felt his smile in the darkness. "You do. Can I kiss you, Eris?"

She hadn't expected him to ask permission. She'd thought he'd charge in, all alpha male dominance and take what he wanted, so to be asked instead put her on the back foot.

"Yes. Yes, you can," she found herself answering, holding her breath as he leaned down. His lips brushed hers in the softest kiss, all butterfly exploration, and her hands bunched on the fabric of his t-shirt.

He tilted his head, brushing his tongue against her full lower lip. Heat spiraled through her as she opened automatically for him. A soft growl rumbled up from the center of his chest as he took her invitation, deepening the kiss in a tangle of tongues and a blaze of heat.

She stopped thinking as he plundered her mouth with devastating finesse. All that mattered was him and how he made her feel... all that mattered was he kept kissing her like this. Whimpering, she pressed closer, and his hand slid down from the small of her back. He cradled her ass as she half climbed him like a tree, wrapping her leg around his hip and moaning as she rocked against him, the prominent bulge in his pants pressed right where she needed it.

He broke away on a gasp, lips a hairsbreadth from hers. With a soft moan, he leaned his forehead against hers.

"Much as I am desperate to continue, this is not the time or the place, beautiful. Let's get out of here, get someplace safe, and then I plan to worship every inch of your body until you pass out with pleasure."

❖

She shivered and nestled against him. Zero didn't think his heart had ever been so full or his cock so fucking hard.

He held her tenderly against the larger bulk of his body, his hand smoothing over her lower back. She was tiny compared to him, full of curves. His onboard also registered the curviness of her form, giving him statistics on her likely fitness levels and stamina in the back of his mind. He ignored the stream of data with the ease of long practice and concentrated on holding her.

Then he moved slightly, tucking his fingers under her chin to make her look up at him. He'd caught the wince at the comments from the men outside.

"When we get to safety, you're going to explain 'tin can' to me," he rumbled softly.

She shrugged, not bothering to hide the hurt in her eyes because she assumed he couldn't see her clearly. His heart ached for the resignation that wrapped around that hurt and rage that surged through him, urging him to break free from the closet and storm after those men. Kill them for daring to hurt her.

"It's a derogatory nickname for my old unit," she

shrugged. "I was Armored Infantry... We weren't popular. Other troops thought we stole their jobs."

"Uh-huh... assholes." He made a note to check into the Armored Infantry when they were free and clear. It hadn't been on her station record, just that she'd been medically discharged from her species' military. He obviously needed to dig a little deeper.

Warning, his onboard spoke in the back of his mind. *Remaining in place increases the chance of discovery by 9.73% per minute, rising to 93.74% after fifteen minutes.*

"We need to get out of here. Ready to move?" he asked, dragging her out of possible bad memories of the past.

She drew in a deep breath and nodded. "We need to get off the station. Is your ship still here?"

He shook his head. "Nope. They traveled onward to Praxis-Four. We're going to have to make our own way. As soon as we're off station, I'll signal them to double back and rendezvous with us."

Approval filled him as she nodded briskly at the new information. There were no hysterics or panic at the news the easy way off Tarantus—his ship— was a no-go. She simply moved on to the next problem.

"Okay, we need to secure a ship. I'm assuming my

credentials will be wiped and the facial recog systems on the station will pick me up as soon as we move." She bit at her lower lip and his gaze riveted to it. The need to kiss her again filled him, but he fought it back. He needed to focus, or they were already dead.

"I can handle the facial recog." He was already in the systems. Altering the recognition pattern so her biometric data matched that of a woman in her mid-fifties who had died several years ago was the work of a moment. It was a quick and dirty hack that wouldn't last long before it was discovered, but they didn't need long. They only needed long enough to get off this damn rust-bucket of a station.

"How?" She started to ask but then shook her head. "Not important. Let's move. If we can get down to the lower docks, we have a chance. The security feeds are always glitchy down there. If we pick one of the smaller transports... we might be able to jack it before its owners get back... oh fuck," she looked at him, stricken. "We're about to become fucking pirates."

He shrugged, easing her away from him and moving to open the door. "Not my first rodeo, won't be my last."

5

*E*ris followed her knight in black combats out of the cleaning closet. As they emerged, one of the cleaning bots cheeped and left its charging pod to slide down the tracks to the floor.

She put her foot in front of it to stop it as she unclipped her ID bracelet and dropped it in the waste receptacle on the top. Stepping back, she grinned at Zero as she let it continue on its way.

"Let them chase their damn tails for a while."

He pulled her close, claiming her lips in a swift, hard kiss. "That's my girl."

She flushed at the comment and being called his girl. Even though she was *way* too old to be considered a girl and she'd always argued against any of that kind of possessive nonsense from any guy before... with Zero it was different. At his words a warmth spread from the center of her chest, and she followed him as he set off down the hall.

Within minutes, though, it became apparent they'd underestimated how easy it would be to get down to the docking arms and hijack a ship. Every route they tried was blocked by a group of armed men.

"How many of these fuckers are there?" she hissed, peeking around the corner to check out the group they'd almost walked smack-bang into.

Clad in black body armor like the rest, they carried the latest KT-X assault rifles but wore no unit or regiment badges. Despite that, they were clearly military. The way they moved said they couldn't be anything other than special forces.

Her eyes narrowed. She was a security chief on a backwater station in the ass-end of beyond. Who wanted her dead badly enough to send special forces after her? Someone had their wires crossed somewhere for sure.

But, a clerical error of epic magnitude or not, she couldn't exactly complain to management, not with a dead-or-alive bounty on her head. She flattened herself against the wall and looked at Zero, trying like hell not to panic.

"We'll double back," he said. "I have an idea."

At least one of them did. She nodded, and they turned to head back down the corridor. The station was in complete lockdown with no one around as they made their way to the lower-level habitat sector. None of the lodgings on the station could be considered luxurious, but the lower levels tucked in behind the docking arms were the lowest of the low. Even the cockroaches preferred to live higher up.

"What are we doing here?" she hissed as he paused by a door and hammered on it with a massive fist.

"Fuck off, Zero!" a muffled voice came from inside.

Zero winked at her and leaned in, one massive shoulder against the door. "Either open the door, Sparky, or I'll tear it off its fucking hinges!" he yelled.

The door cracked open widely enough for them to see one blue eye. Jayce Allen. She should have known. "Good luck. It's a slider," he hissed. "Now fuck off. You're messing with my meditation."

The door started to slide shut, but Zero was quicker. Jamming his metal hand into the gap, the door mechanism squealed in protest as he forced it open.

"Meditation?" she asked as Zero ushered her through the door, only letting go when they were both through. The door slid shut behind them and she turned to look at Allen's quarters. Far from the squalid hovel she'd expected, it was neat. Like barracks neat. The blanket on the single bunk was tight enough to bounce a coin off... if you could find such an antique all the way out here.

"I find a little one-on-one time with the captain works most issues out." He gestured toward the bottle of whiskey on the desk. Captain Jones... the cheapest rot-gut whiskey there was on base. She knew it well.

He folded his arms over his chest, looking at them both, and glared at Zero. "What do you want, big guy?"

"Whatever weaponry you got, the keys to whatever ship you can steal and a winning lottery ticket."

Sparky's eyebrow lifted. "What color would you like your dragon? Because if you think you're getting off this rust bucket with SO13 here, you'd better think again."

"Shit..." Eris breathed. "I *thought* they were normal special forces."

SO13 weren't just special forces; they were black ops... blacker than a black cat in a damn coal cellar.

So black they were a myth because most people who saw them didn't survive the encounter.

"Nope," Sparky's lips compressed into a thin line. "So whatever it is, big guy. Not my problem."

Zero didn't move, arms folded over his chest as he mirrored Allen's stance. "Well, I'm making it your problem. Unless you want to be on the Warborne's shit list."

Eris felt like she was watching tennis as she looked between the two men. Uppermost in her mind was the fact that Allen had recognized SO13. Then...

"The Warborne?" she asked, confused.

"My unit," Zero answered without looking away from Allen. The two were locked into a staring contest so intent that if a fly flew between them it was sure to explode. "And you humans owe us. We helped you with Lady Cole. Remember?"

"I *knew* it!" she hissed. He was military, just as she'd suspected. "What... wait? Us *humans?*"

"Yeah," Allen drawled. "Loverboy here didn't tell you? He and his buddies are little green men. Not local. AKA not fucking human. And why do I gotta pay for that mess? Cole was nothing to do with me."

Fuck. This hadn't been how Zero had wanted Eris to finally figure out he wasn't human. But, caught in a staring contest with Sparky, he couldn't reassure her. He winced internally, waiting for her to blow up or issue the barrage of questions he knew was coming.

What he did not expect was for her to round on Sparky. "The fact that you recognized they're SO13 is interesting. Don't'cha think, Allen? It is to me anyway... how would they react if someone were to tell them you were on base as well?"

Oh fuck... she had him there. Zero suppressed his grin as Sparky's expression went flat under his scowl and his eyes shuttered. It was only the tiniest tell, the minutest movement of muscle. For Zero, the human might as well have hung out a banner that Eris had surprised him.

Sparky sighed, running a hand through his shock of dirty blond hair.

"Well, okay... I guess I should welcome you to the dark side then." Then he grinned salaciously and looked Eris up and down. "I'd offer you more than cookies, but lover boy here would turn me into human jam on a bulkhead, so the best I got is the cap'n there..." he jerked his thumb toward the bottle on the desk.

"When we're free and clear of this place, we'll

join you in finishing the bottle," she replied, offering her hand.

Sparky shook it firmly, winking at Zero. "Well, *we* will... Handsome here can't get drunk."

"Oh?" She looked over her shoulder at Zero.

He shrugged, folding his arms so he didn't deck Sparky for daring to touch her. Jealousy was a bitch, surging out of nowhere and almost overwhelming all his systems.

"My non-organic systems purge any poisons before they can become harmful." Shit. He didn't want to explain further than that, not without a lot of preparation and sounding her out. The last thing he wanted was for her to see him as a machine... or worse, a robot. He was a man with a man's needs...

"Fuck... that sucks." Her expression was full of sympathy but leveled out as she looked back at Sparky.

He was pleased to see she let go of the human's hand at the earliest opportunity and stepped back closer to him. The move might have been purely instinctive to put some space between her and the human male, but Zero was more than happy to construe it as she wanted to be closer to him. That she trusted *him*.

He wanted her to trust him. He wanted her to do

far more than trust him... but trust was a start and could go so many exciting places.

"Okay... show us the goodies," Eris ordered, all professional and business-like. Only she wasn't. Her heart rate and respiration were elevated. Zero knew the signs. She was riding the edge of panic and was concealing it well. "So... what you got in the line of weaponry?"

Sparky nodded and turned. Reaching under the bunk, he pulled free a trunk and opened it. It was filled with weapons—from assault rifles to lethal-looking trench-knives. Eris whistled softly.

"Well, guess we know who's been keeping the gun-runners on base busy. Don't we?"

Sparky chuckled, already beginning to arm up. The way he moved, strapping weaponry to his body in various holsters and sheaths... yeah, him having been military made complete sense.

"Always better to have and not want than need and not have. That's what my momma always said anyway."

"I'm not sure what's scarier..." Zero quipped, selecting a pump-action shotgun and a couple of vicious blades to add to his handguns. "You having a mother, or that she might be like you."

Sparky grinned. "Nah, you got it backward,

squire. Chip off the old block, me. Apart from the fact she's scarier. I'm a teddy bear compared."

"Yeah, that's what scares me." Zero moved to the door, un-focusing his eyes for a moment so he could concentrate on the corridor outside. If the troops aboard were as good as Sparky claimed, it wouldn't take them long to figure out they'd been duped and start clearing the station level by level. "So... ship?"

Fully armed with body armor in place, Sparky slid a flexi from his pocket and flicked it on. "May I suggest the *Aegis,* currently on docking arm fifteen... she's a heavy freighter who usually runs cargo to the Terra-Nova systems."

Eris looked up at him sharply. "Pirate territory?"

He nodded. "Aye. Which means they're gonna be packing decent shields and rail-guns despite the fact they're listed as unarmed."

"Good point. Okay... fifteen isn't far from here." She reached over and flicked the screen to a view of the station. "If we head down through these sectors here and here... a service elevator here is always listed as out of service, but I have the override codes for it."

"Not yours, I take it?" Sparky asked quickly. "'Cause, sorry to break it to you, but thirteen will have locked everything of yours down six ways to Sunday, sweetheart."

She gave him a hard look. "Do you take me for a fucking idiot? Of course it's not mine. I memorized the chief engineer's codes the last time I went down there with him."

"Smart," Zero commented to get their attention. "Corridor's clear outside. We should move now before they start a level-by-level search."

Sparky locked and loaded his assault rifle. "After you, big guy."

If anyone had told Eris yesterday she'd be trying to escape the station with an alien cyborg and an ex-con, she'd have laughed them off the damn thing. But here she was, creeping down the corridor hoping like hell they didn't run into a team of the scariest special-forces soldiers in the known galaxy.

"Hang left. Tangoes coming down the right-hand corridor," Zero said quietly behind her.

He'd been keeping up a quiet commentary, guiding them through the station corridors as they headed toward docking arm fifteen. Three times they'd had to double back or wait. She didn't need to tell either of them that the frequency and number of enemy patrols weren't a good sign. From the tone of

Zero's voice and the grim expression on Allen's face as he took point and then held position to cover them as they moved, both already knew.

They took the left corridor but halfway down Zero hissed. "Fuck, they doubled back."

They froze in place in the middle of the corridor. She and Allen covered opposite sides of the hallway.

"Which way, big man?" Allen asked, voice terse. "We really don't want to be caught here. They'll cut us to fucking ribbons."

She didn't take her eye off the corridor in front of her, finger coiled around the trigger. As soon as anything moved on her side, she was ready to toast it.

"No direct route to the docking arm... shit... there's too many," Zero growled. "We'd need a tank to get through."

"Taking point," she said abruptly, moving out of position as Zero took her place at the back of the group. "Got a plan."

Two corridors later, they walked into hell. As they were halfway down, they heard yelling behind them.

"*Contact rear!*" Sparky bellowed, already returning fire.

Half her brain paused to admire the way he

moved. The joker disappeared, and in his place was a lethal soldier, his rifle barking as he cut down the commandoes filling the corridor behind them with a deadly aim.

She and Zero joined the fray, and she lost herself in the rhythm of battle. *Aim, fire, move... take cover, aim, fire. Move...* Over and over. She ran out of ammo for her primary weapon, so she discarded it, going to the handguns she'd holstered to her hips.

"Where the hell are we going?" Sparky demanded as she led them down to the storage units. "We can't hide in one of these, they're not shielded. We'll be sitting ducks."

"Just hold the line," she ordered. "Buy me a couple of minutes. That's all I need."

She didn't wait for an answer as she placed her weapon by Zero's knee and sprinted down the corridor. Keeping low, she ran fast and tried to stay in cover as much as she could. Still, the skin between her shoulder blades itched. Any moment she expected to catch a bullet between them. Which would suck. After everything she'd been through, she didn't intend to buy it in a scratty storage area on a rust bucket like Tarantus.

She skidded to a halt in front of her storage unit and punched her access number in. Her fingers slipped on the pad, and the screen bleeped an error code at her.

"Fuck!" she hissed, sweat trickling down her spine as she concentrated. She needed to get the numbers right. Three wrong tries and she'd be locked out. If that happened, they were fucked. Six ways to Sunday. Without lube.

She tapped numbers again. Every second out of cover, her survival instincts screamed at her.

"Code confirmed. Access granted," the smooth voice of the computer announced. The door opened with a hiss of compressed air and a heavy clunk.

She pushed at it, sliding through the gap as soon as it was wide enough. A hiss escaped her as she scraped the skin off her side on the way. Then she was through, almost falling onto the floor in the unit. Scrambling to her feet, she launched herself toward the tank suit at the back.

Reaching it, she slapped her hand on the quick-release plate in the center of the chest. It registered her print and unfolded with a hiss of hydraulics. Not wasting a second, she hauled herself up and into the cockpit with practiced grace.

Sliding into place, she started powering up the suit even as it closed around her.

"Armored suit series three-zero-seven online.

Calibrating for operator... lower limb obstruction present. Please advise."

"Shit!"

She shoved at the closing panels to hold them open while she leaned down. Pulling the dagger from the sheath on her tac rig, she cut her pant leg off and ripped the exoskeleton free. It clattered to the deck in front of the suit as the panels closed.

"Obstruction removed. Recalibrate and align with neural implants," she ordered, checking the power levels and bringing the weapons systems online.

"Calibrating... neural implants location, aligning to operator nervous system... warning, nervous system damage detected. Warning. Operating this unit may cause further damage."

"Fucking bullets will cause further damage!" she hissed, punching buttons. "Override. Initiate link anyway."

"Link initiated.... Confirmed. Engage upper torso systems?"

Her lower body was locked into place, and the breath escaped her lungs as she felt the familiar prickle of the suit interfacing with her neural implants. Making sure her harness was secured, she slipped her arms into the arms of the suit. The clamps wrapped around her arms just above the elbow and over her wrists. She reached out and took hold of the controls.

"Engage upper torso systems now," she confirmed. "Close unit and armor up. Going weapons hot."

The last panel slid into place over her head, covering her face, her heads up display flickering to life on her side of the transparent panel. Pushing the unit into motion, she strode across to the door, her metal "feet" clunking on the deck.

She rolled her shoulders and arms, making the guns on her shoulders—both machine and plasma —turn on their mounting to ensure she had full firing arcs.

"Confirm weapons hot," the suit replied. "Targeting systems active."

She nodded, bringing her current ammunition levels up to display in the corner of her screen. Not one hundred percent, but she wouldn't need it for this. They had to get to the docking arm.

Her lips compressed as she reached the door, ducking down to step out into the corridor. The air was alive with bullets and energy bolts, both pinging off her armor as she turned to see Zero and Sparky pinned in place at the end of the corridor.

"Computer, acquire enemy targets," she ordered calmly, waiting the fraction of a second for the computer to lock on. Then she rolled her shoulders again and bellowed.

· "*Take cover!*"

6

Zero had been in combat as long as he could remember.

Sure, his memory only stretched back as far as T'Raal digging him out of the wreckage of that shuttle in the ass-end of beyond, severely wounded. Even without any memory of what had gone before, his body told the tale of a lifetime of violence. Scars... Evidence of repaired damage in his physical and cybernetic systems. Unit tattoos that didn't match anything on record in any known galaxy or species military.

In other words, he'd been a soldier all his life. Somewhere. And since then, he'd fought with the Warborne against some of the most dangerous and brutal enemies out there.

But he couldn't remember any of them being quite so determined and tenacious as the humans firing on them right now. It was all he and Sparky could do to stop their opponents overrunning their position at the end of the corridor to buy Eris the time she needed.

But where the fuck was she?

He didn't have time or chance to look over his shoulder the way she'd run. She had a plan. He had to trust that. She wouldn't have cut and run, leaving them here to die... No, she wouldn't have. She wasn't built that way.

He might not have known her for long, and he might not know her as well as he wanted just yet, but he *knew* her. Knew the kind of person she was. Like him, she was a soldier through and through.

Which meant she wasn't the kind of person to leave her comrades to die.

"Will you lot just fucking *fuck* off and fucking die?" Sparky bellowed as he and Zero fired in concert, laying down a lethal net of suppressive fire. But despite it, despite their combined training and experience, the black-armored humans were creeping closer. It was only a matter of time.

Odd noises sounded behind them—whirring and heavy clunking that sounded like footsteps. If there were eight feet instead of two, he could almost imagine a *drakeen* approaching to back them up. Gods, what he'd do for one of the heavy-duty combat bots right about now. It would easily cut a swathe through the humans in front of them, and they could use it as cover when they moved forward.

"*Take cover!*"

The voice was mechanized, female, and came from behind them. Zero and Sparky both hit cover at the same time, heads ducked as the air around them filled with bullets and energy fire the like of which he'd never seen before.

"What the fuck?" he murmured, turning just as Sparky whooped.

"Fuck me! She's a tanker!"

His jaw dropped as he turned. A behemoth of a machine walked toward them, guns on its shoulders recoiling in their rails as it fired mechanically, cutting down the humans trying to kill them. His thoughts of a *drakeen* hadn't been too far off the mark. Bipedal, it was a hulking brute and heavily armored. Bullets from the humans pinged off it in showers of sparks. He could just see Eris's face through a screen on the thing's chest.

"*Get behind me!*" she ordered, her voice strange and distorted as she walked toward them.

"Tanker?" he asked Sparky as the two of them ran low and fast, getting behind the bulk of the machine she drove. As they moved, he caught a glimpse of her name painted on the breastplate.

"Armored Infantry Unit!" Sparky yelled, falling in behind Eris's leg and using the machine as cover as he started to fire back at the humans. He explained between bursts of firing, "Basically portable tanks. They were decommissioned about a decade ago. I didn't think any were left. These things are antiques now!"

"*Moving left!*" she warned them. They adjusted their movement, staying behind her as she pushed the human forces up while backing into the corridor that would lead them toward the docks. Only a few humans were left now, and it took the work of a minute for Eris to pick them off.

"Okay, we need to move. Not much power left."

They broke into a run, Zero and Sparky taking point as Eris covered the rear. With the increased firepower, the resistance they met along the way was minimal and quickly dealt with.

"There she is," Sparky nodded toward the airlock as they emerged onto the docking arm. "The *Aegis*. You might wanna do your thing, big man. You'll be quicker than me cracking her security systems."

"Make it quick," Eris advised, clunking to take a position in the center of the corridor while facing the central station. Her guns rotated and reset in their rails, covering the passage. "*We got incoming!*"

Without the need to check on the station security feeds, Zero instead dove into the system. Freezing in place, he concentrated on racing through cyberspace. Data flowed past him in its rawest form, constructs for different departments, routines, and subroutines blooming like flowers in a garden. He ignored them all, searching for what he needed. He raced along the data stream like it was a highway until the construct that was the *Aegis* rose up in front of him like a mountain rising from the deep.

Skidding as he changed direction, he raced for it, his data-self already analyzing the shape and form of its defenses. It was more complicated than he'd thought and would be hard to hack. If only he was a... the memory glitch hit him out of the blue, the thought incomplete. If only he was a what?

Shaking his head, he ignored it. Every so often his systems would reach for information that wasn't quite there. Like an idea that was on the tip of his tongue, but as soon as he reached for it, it vanished like early morning mist in the sun.

He didn't have the finesse to break the *Aegis*

systems covertly, not at this speed. Instead, he changed his digital form and sped up. Like a battering ram, he hit the ship's firewall at full speed. There was a moment of profound digital silence, a freeze-frame in the flow of data. Then it tumbled down around him in a cascade effect that allowed him to surge forward and take control.

"I'm in," he announced, hitting his body with a rush and surging into motion toward the airlock. Sparky moved with him, Eris still firing at the human forces that had appeared in the corridor while he'd been out. He realized the human had been covering him with his own body.

Humans... they were the strangest things.

"Fuck me. That was fucking weird. You were here, but you weren't there!" Sparky turned and fired as they ran, even as Eris walked backward, keeping the human forces off their backs. "I thought I was fucking god with a keyboard, but you're something else. Aren't you?"

"You'd better believe it." He winked, shoving Sparky ahead of him into the airlock. Even without his body armor, he could still take a fuckload more damage than a human. "Taking control of the ship now. Cycling the engines up. *Eris, get your metal ass in here now!*"

The two men fired from the cover of the airlock as Eris cut and ran, her steps reverberating through the deck beneath their feet. Shouts rang out behind her as bullets pinged off her armored back.

"*Shut the lock!*" she ordered, her face grim behind the screen. "*I'll make it!*"

He nodded, ignoring the screams from his protective male side as he hit the controls. If she didn't make it... he shut the thought down, firing back as the door started to slide down, cutting off his view of the corridor. His heart pounded. Eris was still too far away.

"Shit, she's not going to make it," he hissed, reaching out to slam into the controls to open the lock again. A hand shot out, wrapping around his wrist with surprising strength. Sparky shook his head.

"She'll make it, squire. Believe me. Those tankers are fucking hard bitches to put down."

"They'll kill her!" Zero hissed, yanking his arm away and going for the control. But before he could hit it, he heard a screech of metal on metal. Then Eris's tank suit appeared under the door, sliding across the deck into the airlock. She'd barely cleared it when it slammed shut inches from her "head."

"Told ya!" Sparky winked and patted the

armored chest. "Good on you, girl. Now you wanna get your lazy ass up off the floor? We still gotta get this tub outta here."

"Yeah, yeah... keep your fucking hair on," Eris replied, lying still in the suit. She hadn't been in combat for years, and she could tell. Every cell in her body ached from operating the suit even for that small amount of time. "Need to shut this baby down. I'll catch up."

The two men nodded and then were gone, leaving her on her own. She closed her eyes and sighed in relief. Alone, she didn't have to hide the pain on her face. *Shit.* She really should have taken this thing out for a spin a time or two to keep her skill levels up.

But...

"Neural link lost to lower right limb," the suit warned her. *"Recalibrating."*

And there it was. The implants in her leg had finally burned out. A tear leaked from the corner of her eye and rolled down her cheek as she spoke, her voice thick. "Cancel recalibration and initiate shutdown."

"Warning: optimal position for storage not achieved.

Please confirm shutdown."

"Confirmed. Initiate shutdown."

"Affirmative. Shutdown procedure initiated."

She felt the suit release her, going dead and inert as the front panels opened. Taking a deep breath, she started to haul herself up and out of the thing. Her right leg was useless, as dead as the suit, trailing behind her as she moved.

With a heave, she rolled herself up and over the head of the unit. All operators practiced and practiced the movement in case their suits got snarled in something and they needed to make a quick exit. It gave them cover if they needed to operate the shoulder weapons from behind.

She landed hard, a hiss escaping her as she fought to keep her feet. Her right leg was utterly useless, the left not far behind it. Holding herself up with a hand on the edge of the open suit, she looked around for something to use as a crutch.

"Wherever you are, beautiful, hold onto something," Zero's voice came over the ships comm. "Going engines hot."

"Warning: Inner airlock doors open." The ship's computer informed her. *"Warning: Inner airlock doors open."*

Abandoning her search, she held onto the suit

for dear life. Not a moment too soon. Less than a second later, the deck lurched, the roar of the engines assaulting her ears as they burned fuel to get away from the station. Down here she was blind to what was going on, so she closed her eyes and hoped the outer airlock doors held.

The next half-minute of her life was lost to deafening noise and fervent prayer. She didn't know anything about the *Aegis,* hadn't seen the logs... how was she to know if the engineering team kept up their maintenance schedules?

Grimly, she focused on something else— anything else—to take her mind off the precarious situation she was in. Like the way Zero had held her... The hardness of his body against hers, the satin-over-steel of his skin, and the way he kissed her, like she was the only woman in the universe. She closed her eyes and concentrated on the memory as hard as she could. Just a little longer. If she survived this, she was taking him up on his offer of making her pass out from pleasure.

He was so intense. Over everything. What would it be like to be the focus of that intensity? Just the thought made her shiver, heat washing through her. If she wasn't holding onto her suit for grim death, she'd have gone all weak at the knees.

Then, as soon as it had started, the noise and rattling surfaces around her cut out to leave blessed silence.

"Thank fuck," she murmured, making her way around the suit and using it to keep herself upright. She couldn't feel her right leg, but for now, it seemed to be working. As long as she concentrated. It wouldn't last long, though. She knew that. It was a last gasp, the implants firing sporadically to power the movement. The only way she knew that was because the muscles in the back of her calf, bared by her cutaway pants, were jumping like a box of frogs.

She needed to be sitting down when they finally gave out. That or she'd sit her ass down on the deck without warning, and she'd rather not suffer that indignity in front of her new crewmates. She'd rather explain the situation to them than give them a front-row demonstration as to how useless she'd just become.

Pushing off from the suit, she made it to the door of the airlock, clinging to it as she shuffled through to the right side. Breathing heavily, she triggered the inner doors.

"Sorry, old girl. I'll come to fetch you soon," she promised as the doors rolled shut and sealed. Only then did she allow herself a sigh of relief. At least she was no longer at risk of sucking cold hard space because someone cut corners with the repair routine.

"HEAD FOR THE PHEIDIAN BELT," Sparky, in the copilot's seat, advised as he brought the guns and tactical systems online. Zero concentrated on the propulsion systems, spoofing traffic control clearance to get the clamps to disengage and then dropping the *Aegis* out of the docking cradle.

As soon as they were clear, he gunned the engines, the punch of g-forces pushing them both back in their seats. Part of his mind worried about where Eris was. If she was in the corridors, he hoped she'd found something to hold onto.

"Think we got them on the hop, big guy," Sparky kept up a constant stream of chatter while Zero kept his focus on getting them clear of the station. The *Aegis* systems were a little different than what he was used to but nothing he couldn't handle. Bringing the star charts online, he located the Pheidian Belt.

"Course set. Burn in three, two, one... Burn initiated," he announced, his voice a combination of his own and the measured digitized tones of the ship's computer. "Did any of them follow us?"

Sparky kept his eyes on the tactical screens, slowly shaking his head. "I don't think so." He motioned with his hands, bringing up a close view of the station, now rapidly dwindling behind them. He focused in on a large, bulky ship on docking arm four.

"SO13 standard transport. I *may* have revoked their clearance to leave," he winked up at Zero. "And thrown in a shelter-in-place admiralty order just for kicks and giggles. It should take them a couple of hours to figure that out. By then, we'll be in the belt, and they can't track us."

"Sparky, you are one scary son of a bitch!" Zero whooped, levering himself out of his chair. With the ship on autopilot, he could indulge in his need to find Eris and make sure she was okay.

"Hey! My mom resembles that remark!" the human threw back as Zero left the bridge.

He was still uplinked to the ship's computer, enough to monitor most of what was going on, so it didn't matter exactly where he was onboard. He couldn't control everything, though... the reason he needed to track Eris down himself... and again that feeling of something wrong with his onboard assaulted him.

No, not wrong...

He frowned as a new fragment of information emerged from the shattered mess of his long-term memories... the place that the nightmare came from. His onboard was functioning correctly, but it just wasn't the right *type* for controlling a whole ship all by himself. He wasn't built for that, his specialty was...

And the knowledge slipped away again. He hissed in frustration. He'd almost had it then—so close he could practically taste it.

The frustration disappeared in a heartbeat as he turned the corner and spotted Eris. His immediate reaction was to smile, pleasure to see her rolling through him. But then his expression fell flat as he saw the way she was clinging to the wall. She had a look of pain on her face, and something seemed to be wrong with her leg.

"*Shit.* Sweetheart, what happened?"

He was across the space that separated them in a heartbeat to sweep her up in his arms. If she'd been injured because of him—because she hadn't been strapped in when they took off—he'd never forgive himself.

She didn't complain, though tears pooled in her eyes as she curled up trustingly against his chest. His heart, both organic and cybernetic, stopped at those tears. Eris Archer was a strong woman... to see her so broken was a shock to the system.

"Please," she whispered against his neck. "Get me to medbay."

7

"What happened? Did you fall... shit, was it during acceleration? Oh fuck, sweetheart, I am so sorry. I should have waited until I knew you were secure."

The self-recrimination in Zero's voice almost broke her heart as the big cyborg gathered her into his arms and practically ran toward the medbay. She clung to him, hiding her face against the strong column of his throat, and prayed for the strength to get it together before they reached their destination.

"We're here. Don't worry. Everything's going to be okay," he promised her, laying her down on the examination bed in the middle and then looking around at the equipment. For the first time since she'd known him, he looked lost... bewildered.

"Fuck! I need Talent."

She shook her head, pointing to the medication cabinet. "Nope. You don't need special skills or to be a doctor. Just get me some painkillers and a neuro-stim; they should be in there."

Her voice tightened as a wave of agony washed up over her, her abused nervous system letting her know there was a problem. Like a baby, it didn't have words, so screaming was its only option. If she could just get the pain to dull down a little, she could think and then try and figure out what to do.

"No. I mean... Talent's the Warborne's doc," he explained, shoving a hand through his close-cropped hair.

"Meds!" she hissed to remind him.

"Oh shit, yeah. On it." His voice was clipped as he practically tore the door off the medication cabinet and located what she needed.

"Terran is a fucking awful language," he told her as he returned. "But thankfully simple. Interfacing with the medical systems now."

"You do that, handsome," she nodded, grabbing the medication from his outstretched hand. Ripping the lids off, she jammed the injectors against her neck and sighed in relief as the high-strength drugs hit her system. The stim worked through her body, her abused nervous system flaring to life. She hissed and gritted her teeth to ride the wave out.

Zero stood next to her, his large hand enveloping hers and his expression concerned. But his eyes were slightly unfocused for a few seconds before they snapped back, and he looked at her.

"I need to do a full scan," he told her, letting go of her hand. "We need to see what kind of damage we're looking at and then treat you."

As he stepped away, she reached out and grabbed his hand.

"There's no need," she told him desperately.

The last thing she wanted was to appear weak in front of him. And yeah... Well, what guy would want to stick around for a crippled woman? Once he knew, she wouldn't see him for dust... or worse, she'd see the same kind of pity in his eyes she saw in every medic and doctor when they figured out what had happened to her.

"It's fine. I read the manual." He patted her hand in reassurance. "The scans are perfectly safe. I promise."

As much as she tried to keep him with her, he easily disengaged his hand and stepped away.

Sighing, she dropped her head back and closed her eyes. The familiar hum of the scanner filled the air.

"You..." Surprise colored Zero's deep voice. "You have implants?"

She opened her eyes to stare at the ceiling squares above. "Yup. All tank operators do. Sixteen implants with a full neural net to interface with our suits."

"Uh-huh. I can see them. The technology is crude." His voice rang with disgust. "Fucking assholes shouldn't have messed with things they didn't understand."

Anger rose. "Fuck off, my implants are..." *were* "cutting edge. And what would you know about it anyway?" she demanded.

A metal hand appeared in her field of vision, and the fingers wiggled.

"Wanna rephrase that?"

She hissed. Asshole. "Okay, they were cutting edge for *humanity.* I'm assuming your fancy-dancy alien technology is far better."

He grumbled in the back of his throat. "It wouldn't damage the host like this for sure. Shit, your right leg is toast. I'm surprised it didn't cook the limb. Your left leg isn't much better."

"Yeah... I know. They said my next mission

would be my last." She closed her eyes, refusing to allow the tears to stream down her cheeks. He knew now. Knew the damage was permanent. After the stim wore off, she probably wouldn't walk again.

"*What?*" he demanded. "You *knew* this would happen? And you still got into the suit?"

She jumped at the anger in his tone, opening her eyes to find him looming over her. "Why the fuck would you do that?"

Eris had never seen Zero angry before, not even when they'd been facing down the worst of the worst special forces troops trying to kill them. If anything, he'd just seemed slightly amused at the bullets slicing through the air around them and dispatched any that got into his sights with lethal efficiency. But now that calm, joking man was gone and in his place was a towering tsunami of fury.

She looked away, unable to meet his eyes. A large hand slammed into the exam bed by her head.

"For fuck's sake, woman, *look at me!*" he ordered, his voice little more than a snarl. He didn't move, looming half over her as she lay on the bed, his blue eyes cutting like lasers when she lifted hers.

His anger made her shiver, but only a little. Even though he was killing mad, the tiny veins in his temple pulsing, she wasn't scared of him. Far from it. Instead, she was aware of every inch of him. Every hard plane of muscle, the strength in his corded arms as he leaned over her. The full, kissable softness of his lips as he glared down at her.

All she wanted to do was sit up and press her lips against his. Divert his attention. As soon as the thought crossed her mind, her body moved to suit thought to action.

THE FEEL of her lips pressing against his surprised Zero and stopped his tirade instantly. The fury still surged through him, but the instant he registered the softness of her lips, it changed, flipping and burning faster than the *Sprite*. Growling, he slid his hand into the hair at the back of her head and crushed her mouth beneath his.

She gasped, and he took advantage, parting her lips with his in a savage kiss before thrusting his tongue within. She didn't stop him, a soft sound of surrender in the back of her throat as her hands bunched in his shirt. Her taste exploded through him again, that little sound getting him hotter and harder than he'd ever been in his life.

Warning, elevated hormonal levels and heart rate,

his onboard announced in the back of his head. *Recommend sexual intercourse to reduce levels.*

No shit. He silenced his onboard and tightened his fist in her hair. Pulling her head back, he kissed along the slender column of her throat. They were hard, almost biting kisses that he couldn't control... that he didn't *want* to control. Hard and fast. He wanted her more than he'd ever wanted a woman in his life.

Pulling back, he looked down at her, and the sultry look in her half-lidded eyes sent a surge of arousal through him. His cock, trapped against the exam bed, jerked savagely.

"Make a choice," he told her, barely recognizing his own voice. "Tell me to go, or I'm going to fuck you right here and now."

"I..." She blinked and wetted her lips. Her eyes were dark with heat and desire.

He groaned, the sound turning to a growl more feral than any sound he'd ever made. "Don't do that or I won't be responsible for my actions."

She shook her head. "But why? In case you missed it, Zero, I'm a fucking cripple. This will not get better. Ever. I'm done."

He pulled back his lips in a soft snarl. "One... do you think I give a crap about whether you can walk or not? One of my original crewmates was embedded in a fucking ship for god's sake. And two... you're like me, a cyborg. We're fucking modular, baby. We can fix you."

"A ship?" She shook her head. "I'm not a cyborg... wait, did you say you can..." The hope in her eyes speared him to the core. "You can *fix* me?"

He nodded, sliding a hand around her waist and pulling her toward him. At the same time, he altered her position, making her sit up. Like a bulldozer, he forced his hips between her thighs. His heart sang as she welcomed him, her hand sliding up the side of his neck as he claimed her lips again.

This kiss was only marginally less bruising than the first. He'd intended to be gentler but didn't have it in him. She was a fire in his blood and he couldn't get enough, would never be able to get enough. He'd suspected it from the moment he'd first seen her, but now he knew for sure. She was *his*.

And he was irrevocably hers.

The kiss went supernova in a heartbeat. He broke away with a gasp to trail kisses along her jaw and down the slender column of her throat. Her hands stroked over his shoulders, pausing for a second as she registered the metal of his shoulder.

He pulled back, stripping the shirt off in less than a second to drop it on the floor behind them.

He didn't say anything, simply watching her face as she took him in. Sitting on the edge of the bed as she was, he couldn't miss how tiny she was compared to him, and a thrill of arousal speared through him. He'd never thought of himself as the sort to find a woman's fragility appealing, but he found he liked being larger and stronger than Eris. He could protect her, look after her... and that fed a need deep inside he hadn't realized he had.

Her face was rapt, her dark gaze flicking to his as he took her hand and pressed it against his shoulder.

"It's okay," he rasped, voice heavy with need. "You can touch it."

"You can feel that?" she whispered, her voice low and intimate, just between them. His cock throbbed at the husky tones and then went into near meltdown as her fingers stroked the join between his skin and the metal of his arm. He managed to nod.

"My cybernetics are as sensitive as human flesh," he was talking but had no idea where the words were coming from. His mouth was merely filling in while his brain was occupied studying the shape of her lips and the beauty of her face. "More onboard sensors as well."

"Good."

She leaned in, her lips brushing against his chest just below the hollow of his throat. He groaned, his head dropping back as she trailed soft kisses along his collarbone. His hand slid through the silken length of her hair, returning to cup the back of her neck gently as she reached his shoulder.

She didn't pause, her kisses continuing across the metal, and he moaned as his lips parted. He'd never had a lover who accepted every part of him so readily. Most just ignored his visible cybernetics and avoided touching them. That she did so without prompting...

He growled again, metal hand sliding to spread out over the back of her hips. He pulled her closer and ground the evidence of his arousal against that part of her he ached to be buried hilt deep in. The movement broke the dam of restraint. He gripped her hair to pull her head back again.

His mouth crashed down over hers, her whimper as she met him kiss for kiss the sweetest damn thing he'd ever heard. He couldn't stop touching her, his hands sliding down her curves and around. His tongue wrapped around hers as he cupped her breasts, a growl of need and approval deep in his throat as he cradled their weight. She was curvy rather than slender and toned, but he didn't care. He loved women in all their shapes and sizes. They were a beautiful mystery to him. Her more than any other.

Breaking away from such a delicious handful, he went for her belt buckle, quickly dealing with the barrier between him and what he wanted. Hand behind her hips, he tilted them to where he wanted her, sliding his left into her pants. She gasped against his lips, pausing to look up at him as he parted her pussy lips with strong fingers.

She was hot and wet, biting her lip as he located her clit. Her hands bit into his shoulders as he began to stroke her, holding her gaze. Heat blazed in her eyes as he teased her, his blunt fingertip smoothing the slick heat he found over the tiny pearl. She gasped, closing her eyes as her hips rocked in reaction.

He growled, wanting to watch her as he brought her to pleasure, and moved, sliding a finger deep into the tight, wet heat of her body's embrace.

And was undone...

"*Fuck!* You're tight," he managed, shoving her chin up with a nuzzle so he could kiss along the underside of her jaw and down her neck below her ear. "I'll take it slow, baby. I promise."

He would have to. There was no way in creation

he would ever hurt her, but... *gods,* it would be awesome. His cock jerked in anticipation, all his male instincts howling at him to get on with it. To spread her out over the exam bed, strip those pants from her and get himself where they both wanted him to be.

Needed him to be.

She nodded, the softest whimper in the back of her throat as she rode his hand. With a grunt of triumph, he pumped slowly, adding a second finger to stretch her gently as he brought his thumb to bear against her clit. Her nails bit into his shoulders, sending his arousal higher and higher. Once he got inside her, he was going to make her scream all night long, maybe all tomorrow night as well...

"Oh god, Zero..." she moaned, her hand sliding up the back of his neck as the other skated down his arm. "That's... I'm... *fuuuck!*"

He felt her climax wash up, the tiny contractions of her body before she clamped down. The rush as her release hit bathed his fingers in more slick heat. Tilting her head, he claimed her lips at the same time, sliding his tongue deep to taste her passion as she shattered apart.

And it was glorious.

Her back arched, her body tight and she clung to

him like he was her only anchor in the entirety of existence. Her kiss was white-hot, sensual as she drowned in pleasure, demanding a response from him that he was more than eager to give as he kept touching and stroking her. He stretched her release out as much and as far as he could until she shivered in his arms and collapsed against him, boneless.

Gently, he pulled his fingers free, still holding her against him. His own body screamed for completion, but he wasn't going to give up the soft trust she placed in him, this moment of togetherness as she lay against him.

"That was…" He tilted her face up to his. "You're beautiful—"

He didn't get the chance to say anymore or even kiss her as the shipwide comm sparked into life, Sparky's voice filling the room.

"Hey, guys. I know you're probably naked and doing it right now, but… we kinda got a problem."

"I FUCKING HATE THAT HUMAN," Zero groaned, resting his forehead against hers.

Eris kept her eyes closed, not wanting to lose the intimacy and closeness of the moment just yet. Her pants were still undone, and Zero's hand on her stomach was a reminder of what they'd done... where it would have gone if they hadn't been cock-blocked by an ex-con.

"Guys?" the comm sparked again. "I'm not fucking about. SO13 are on our tail, and I can't operate this tub alone!"

"Fuck!" Zero's expression was grim as he pulled away. Quickly she fastened her pants as he scooped her up into his arms. "He's right. We've got three on our tail, and there's no way we can outrun them."

"Get me to the bridge," she ordered, a little redundantly because he was already running that way.

She wrapped her arms around his neck and clung to him, knowing he wouldn't drop her. Curiously she looked at him, noting that division of attention again. It was weird. She knew he was right there with her, concentrating on where he was putting his feet... but at the same time, she knew part of him wasn't with her at all. It was somewhere else. Somewhere...

"Are you linked to the ship as well?" she asked softly, knowing he would hear her.

His terse nod was all the answer she needed to confirm that he hadn't been lying about not being human. Given her situation, she'd made sure to keep up with technological advances on the cybernetic front. It had pretty much stalled when the *Scorperio* units had crippled their operators. The furthest doctors would venture these days were things like the exoskeletal supports she'd been forced to rely on over the last few years. She knew beyond a shadow of a doubt that the level of technology he so casually displayed... humanity wasn't anywhere close to it. Obviously, the Lathar were.

They reached the bridge to find Sparky strapped into the copilot's seat. He cast them a look over his shoulder. "Glad you've both got clothes on. Strap in. This is going to be a bumpy ride."

"Put me there," Eris ordered, motioning to the gunner's position. She wasn't surprised to see it. Ships that ran in the Pheidian Belt were often armed to the teeth, a show of force to put off pirates. Hopefully, it would be enough.

"You got it, babe," he murmured, setting her down gently. He reached for her harness to strap her in but she slapped his hands away.

"My legs don't work, not my hands. Now *go!*" she ordered, nodding toward the pilot's chair.

"Yes, ma'am." He stole a quick, hard kiss and was gone.

Her hands were swift and efficient, buckling

herself in as she looked at the screen. To her relief, it was familiar. An *argus* seventeen control unit with what looked like byzantine seven rail guns and, she flicked the screen across... yeah, a full complement of torpedoes. It was just the big brother to the weapons system in her suit, one she'd spent many hours training on.

"Weapons systems coming online," she called out, attention on the tracking systems as they came online. Her expression tightened. Three *lancer* class troop carriers were following them. They were fast, maneuverable and unfortunately armed to the teeth.

"Confirm, three targets coming in hot. I can keep them off our tails but not for long. Gonna need some fancy flying, boys."

"You got it, doll," Sparky replied, and a small lurch told her they'd just disengaged the autopilot.

Sliding her hands into the gun controls, she called out over her shoulder. "Any pearls of wisdom to impart about fighting SO13, Allen?"

"Yeah," he called back. "Don't get fucking shot."

"I had heard that tends to sting a little," she threw back, just as Zero warned. "Going for a high-g right and then prep for flight pattern Alpha-three-three-nine. In three, two, one... *mark!*"

Eris gritted her teeth as the ship rolled, peeling

off to the right. The high-speed maneuver raised a question she filed for later. If Zero wasn't human, how the hell did he know Terran combat patterns so well?

Automatically she adjusted her line of sight, her chair swiveling in its mountings to keep her level as she focused on the ships following them. Working in concert with the targeting systems, she grinned in triumph as two lit up red.

"Torpedoes away," she announced, hitting the triggers. The tail plumes of both torpedoes blossomed in her view screen for a split second. Then the ship pitched and dropped, sliding behind an asteroid just as the lancers engaged their rail guns. Without line of sight, she was forced to rely on her screens.

"Direct hit, one down. One shook the lock," she called out, but then it was game on.

Both Allen and Zero called out flight patterns. She responded on the fly, adapting her firing techniques to the flight profile and the cover from the asteroids around them. They played hide and seek with the lancers, trying to stay in shelter and inflict the maximum amount of damage without getting tagged themselves.

But nothing could last forever.

"Guys," she called out in warning, cutting the rail guns as they slid behind another asteroid. "Running low on ammo. I have maybe two engagements left. We're gonna need to make a break for it. Or we're fucked. Seriously."

❖

8

"Fuck!" Sparky, strapped into the seat next to him, spat. "She's right. And we're almost down to vapor on the fuel. We're out of options, big man. Any ideas?"

Zero's lips compressed into a thin line. He didn't need to check the systems to know they were both telling the truth. As soon as he'd slid into the pilot's seat and taken control, he'd known they had a snowball in hell's chance of beating the three human ships. All they could do was evade and delay the inevitable.

Well... almost all they could do.

"Conserve fuel and ammo," he ordered, adjusting the ship's systems on the fly. Opening airlocks and depressurizing whole areas, he increased efficiency so their fuel would go further. At the same time, he used the long-range sensors to plot a course through the asteroid field. Multitasking was the beauty of being a cyborg. If someone had given him a broom, he could've swept the floor as well.

Then he felt the smallest tickle at the back of his onboard and smiled.

"Eris, I want you to bring the guns to bear on the following coordinates," he ordered, rattling off a sequence in the human format. "Sparky, ready the ship for flight pattern Kilo-seven-five."

Sparky jerked in his seat in surprise, turning to look at him even as he keyed in the sequence. "Sure about that, big man. That's gonna put us flying through a whole fucking heap of rock when shotgun back there blasts that rock to hell. Our shields can't take that load."

"Trust me," Zero shot back. There was no time to explain, so he just gunned the main engines. The instant the little ship shot from its hiding places and into the open, the lancers were on it, a warning tone ringing through the cabin as they got a torpedo lock.

Behind him, Eris bellowed a wordless war cry as she let loose with the guns, the rock in front of them exploding a second before they swung into where it had been at speed.

"We're dead," Sparky whispered. "We're fucking dead. There had better be virgins in heaven or I want a refund."

He felt the tension, the expectation in the air from both humans as they waited for the ship's shields to get shredded by the shrapnel field where the asteroid had been. It was so thick he was surprised any of them could even breathe.

"Hey, Zero," a new voice broke over the comm. T'Raal. "You look like you might be in a spot of bother. Need a hand?"

Zero grinned as the *Sprite* dropped out of high-speed right in front of them, the bigger ship extending its shields to deal with the shattered asteroid. The two ships side-slipped through the field, leaving it between them and the lancers trying to follow.

"Cutting it fine, *Sprite*," he replied aloud for the benefit of the two humans in the cabin. "And yes, we'd welcome a hand here. Got ourselves a couple of dance partners that are a little clingy, if you know what I mean?"

"Yeah, well, Beauty was shopping, so we need to

go back for him. Maintain current course and speed. We'll be right back."

"Roger that. Maintaining current speed and heading."

The Warborne ship wheeled away, using a short hop to take it to the other side of the asteroid field before opening fire.

"My *god*," Eris breathed, leaning forward in her chair to watch the battle on screen. "What kind of weaponry is that thing packing? I've never seen anything like it."

"Little green men," Sparky added wisely. "Although in the Warborne's case, large and not at all green."

"I dunno... sometimes Fin looks a little green around the gills when Red cooks," Zero chuckled, a whole lot more comfortable now the *Sprite* had their backs. He'd never intended to take the *Aegis* all the way. He'd merely wanted to use it long enough to get the Warborne's attention all the way out at Praxis-Four.

"You have a crew member called Beauty?" Sparky leaned on the arm of his chair, watching Zero avidly. "Now either she's a stunner or a ten-pinter. Which is it?"

"Ten-pinter?" For once Zero's innate ability to

decode "human-speak" deserted him and he looked at the tall human blankly.

"Ten-pinter," Eris supplied, shutting down the weapons console. "AKA, a potential sexual partner who requires the intake of a certain amount of alcohol, in this case, ten pints, before they become attractive enough to bed."

Zero's eyebrow winged up toward his hairline. "Ah... pleasant. No, Beauty's neither. In fact, I'm not sure how he got his nickname... his real name is Ilar."

"You all have nicknames?" Sparky demanded. "What's yours? Tinman?"

"Ha-fucking-ha!" Zero flipped him the bird. "Actually, Zero is my nickname. My real name is too long and complicated to be translated correctly."

Not entirely true. He didn't have a name, just a serial number that showed in a tattoo across his cheek if he let it. Not that he planned on telling the piss-taking human that.

"The only one of us who doesn't have one is T'Raal."

"Oh?" Eris asked as he unclipped himself from the pilot's chair. Now they weren't in combat, he didn't need to be there. He could pilot the ship from anywhere. "Why is that?"

He shrugged, heading over to her. Reading his expression, she'd started to unclip herself, reaching her arms up around his neck as he plucked her from her seat. "No idea, just the way it is."

There was a clunk, and the deck shifted sideways a fraction of a millimeter. The humans wouldn't have felt anything but to Zero, it was like a tectonic plate movement.

"How about you ask him yourself?" he suggested and then hid his smile as her arms tightened around his neck, an apprehensive look on her face.

"They're here. Now?"

Eris had never met an actual alien before. Not one that wasn't human in origin anyway. And Zero didn't count because he looked so human she couldn't tell the difference between him and Allen. But as soon as she saw the leader of the Warborne, T'Raal, standing in the airlock, she knew instantly he wasn't human.

"Your eyes were different when you came to Tarantus before," she blurted out as Zero walked across the boarding tunnel between the ships. And they were. On the security footage they'd been blue and human-like. Now, it was like looking into a cat's eyes. No, it was like being studied by a blue-eyed lion on two legs. The man was a predator through and through, of that she was sure.

"Contacts," he replied, an easy smile on his lips. "Welcome aboard the *Sprite*..."

"Eris Archer," she supplied quickly, holding out her hand.

"Eris sustained neural damage operating an armored suit to get us off the station," Zero added. "Her suit needs recovering from the aft airlock and bringing aboard. I'll need Talent... did you manage to get the medbay fixed?"

"We did. Try not to blow it up this time," the large Warborne leader replied with a quirk of his lips. Then his gaze slid past them. "Jayce Allen... why am I not surprised? You're like a magnet for fucking trouble."

"Hey, hey!" The ex-con held his hands up, palms out. "These two found me. I was trying to stay out of it but noooo, they insisted on my help. Probably wouldn't've made it without me."

"Yeah yeah..." Eris broke in as T'Raal motioned them through the door ahead of him, triggering the airlock and tunnel retraction.

"You still didn't explain why you know so much about SO13... or why you ended up in Mirax Ruas," she added, nodding toward the tattoos around his upper arms. Each marked a year in the most brutal prison in the human systems, where life expectancy was less than eighteen months. Anyone with those tattoos was considered a cross between the grim reaper and the bogeyman.

"Crimes against fashion," he supplied promptly, his expression serious. "Apparently spots and stripes don't go together."

She sighed, shaking her head. She should have known she wouldn't get a straight answer from the smart-mouthed ex-con.

"Well," T'Raal said, "welcome aboard the *Sprite*. Sparky, your room assignment is the same. Just don't make too much noise, Red and Fin are back aboard and either of them will squish you like a bug."

Sparky grinned. "You finally got some more crew? Good on you!"

T'Raal sighed, rolling his eyes and shaking his head as the human wandered away up the corridor. "Why I put up with that shit, I have no idea," he groused, making Eris smile.

"I think most people feel that way around him," she commented, waving goodbye as Zero turned and they walked away up the corridor.

She was all eyes, fascinated as she looked about. This was her first alien ship... and it looked a lot like a human one. Only bigger. But then, the Lathar were bigger. Much bigger. Her eyes widened as they reached medbay and she saw the scorch marks on the wall.

"Your boss wasn't kidding about you blowing this place up. Was he?" she whispered to Zero.

Like what she'd already seen of the ship, it was laid out very similarly to a human medical bay. Even though most of the equipment looked odd, she could make a guess as to what it was. But then, a rumor had filtered down through the media that the Lathar were humanity's ancestors. She wasn't sure how accurate that was, but the Lathar *did* seem very human-like at times.

"Nope, he wasn't. We only just managed to get the door closed in time," Zero answered with a grin as he laid her down on one of the beds against the wall. He looked around and whistled lowly. "Although I think we did it a favor. All this equipment is new... and that's a new imperial scanner over there. We had to steal the last one, and none of us knew how to use it."

"Well, that would be the advantage of being mated to the Lord Healer's sister-in-law," a new voice announced from the doorway.

Eris had to shove at Zero as he turned so she

could get a look at the newcomer. Like T'Raal, he was Latharian, his unusual eyes striking, but unlike T'Raal he had short hair.

"Hey there. I'm Talent... the medic on this tub. But call me Tal..." he winked as he approached, offering her his hand. "It sounds a lot less egotistical."

She smiled as she took it, shaking firmly. "Eris Archer. Sta... well, formerly station chief on Tarantus before someone tried to have me killed."

"Yeah, well," the medic replied. "That's just Tuesday around here. You'll get used to it. So... how about you tell me what's going on and I'll see what I can do to help.

"She can't walk," Zero broke in, his expression tight as he glared at their hands. "She already said her hands work just fine. Read me?"

She raised an eyebrow at the possessive comment, but Tal stepped back, a smile on his lips. "Reading you loud and clear. Now... let's see what's going on. Shall we? Lady Archer... you were saying? Did this damage occur when someone on the station tried to kill you?"

She lay back as the alien medic set up equipment around her. "Yes and no. It wasn't the result of a direct hit or injury from enemy forces. I'm a veteran. Medically discharged ten years ago from the armored infantry unit."

"I'm afraid you'll have to treat me like a layperson," Tal responded, shooing Zero away to lean against the wall close by. "My knowledge of Terran military units is sorely lacking. Why were you medically discharged? Were you injured in the line of duty and the battle on the station aggravated old injuries? *That* I can believe. Terran medicine is sorely lacking."

"Medical care in the armored units was state of the art," she argued, her hackles rising at the possible slur. Then she sighed heavily. "Soldiers in the units are enhanced cybernetically to interface with their suits. It's all filament mesh and implanted driver units at the interface points."

Most people just looked blank when she started talking about the science, as much as she understood it, behind her former occupation, but not Tal. Instead, he looked fascinated. "So you found a way to drive the suit using your own body power? Kinetic movement, or... no, the human nervous system doesn't produce enough power to drive anything mechanic..."

"Looks like T'Raal and Red have the suit in the cargo bay now," Zero suddenly announced, his expression distracted again. "Scans are complete if you want to take a look."

"Doing so now." Tal bustled behind a control console for the machine he'd set up around her. She jumped a little as lights flicked on and she was surrounded by rings of light. "If you can lie very still for me, please, Lady Archer. And you," he directed at Zero, "stay the *draanth* away. I had to pull in a *trall* load of favors to get this unit. I don't want it blowing up again. Read me?"

Zero's lips curled. "Loud and clear, Doc. No blowing up your new toys."

Eris hid her grin at the bickering. That was one thing she'd noticed almost immediately about Zero and the Warborne. They had the same kind of camaraderie as in human military units. It made her feel right at home. She watched the rings as they intersected over her head. A combination of white and blue that wasn't quite neon, they were really kind of pretty and emitted a soft, relaxing whoosh as they went past each other.

"Okay... I see the power core in the suit and the way it all connects." Tal's voice had lost its amused note and was now clipped and professional. "What the *draanth* were your doctors thinking? Your implants are screwed, and they've completely *draanthed* your nervous system. There is no way any human system could have taken that kind of load for long."

She shook her head as the rings slowed down. "Nope. It couldn't. Turned out we were never meant to last. Despite all their bullshit and lies, we were a short-term solution to a pressing problem—namely the war in the *Kraxinas* systems. Sol Sector were losing too many troops too fast out there. What with the heavier gravity and brutal terrain, they needed super-soldiers. Tankers were it. Of course, they sold us on it with patriotism and glory... didn't tell us we'd be crippled if we survived. Racked us up... and when one burned out, replaced the operator. We were told it was PTSD when someone got shipped out. They lied."

Zero growled from his position by the wall but she shook her head at him. "Don't worry. I know. We were all plenty pissed and my old captain... last I heard she was getting a class-action suit against them for the shit they didn't tell us."

"We could just find them and nuke the fucking lot of them," Zero offered and she chuckled.

Until she realized he wasn't joking. In fact, neither of the men in the room were smiling as both watched her with unblinking eyes.

"Thanks for the offer, guys, but we've been blocked at every turn. Everything about the *Scorperio* project is classified. Every time Captain Payne gets close..." she shrugged, "suddenly, there's another level of red tape. We can't even get confirmation of names associated with the project, even though I'd *really* like to find out which fuckwit decided it was acceptable to use people like disposable cogs in a machine."

"*You* might not have been able to find out." Tal smiled up from where he stood at the console. "But we specialize in doing shit people don't want us to do. We'll figure it out. But first... we need to get you sorted."

She looked at him in surprise as he moved around the small space, hands swift as he loaded what looked like medication injectors. "Thanks, Tal, but I know it's hopeless," she said, her voice cracking a little. "I was warned long ago I'd end up in a wheelchair. My implants won't even support an exo-support anymore."

Tal's lips quirked as he walked toward her. "Yeah... hopeless for human medicine, maybe. But, in case you hadn't noticed, we're not human. I'm going to give you a couple of shots of cellular enhancer, and then I'll set up the unit for neural reconstruction. We'll see what we can do about these crude implants. Unfortunately, you're going to be stuck in here with me for a few hours."

"Oh woe is me! I don't know how I'll cope." She grinned to take the edge off her words, even though her heart rate had spiked. As friendly as Tal was, this was still a hospital and she'd long since had enough of those.

She tilted her head to allow him to press the injector against her neck. There was a slight pinch, and a hiss as the medication was released into her bloodstream. "Have you ever treated a human before?"

"Hmmmm? Personally, no—"

"What the hell!" Now the machine was off, Zero strode forward from his position against the wall. "You didn't tell me that. I thought there were human women at the Imperial court?"

"You were at the emperor's court?" Eris asked, fascinated. "Isn't that where they took the Sentinel-Five women?"

"There are, and yes, it was," he replied to them both. "But I was not in charge of treating the human females. I'm not a full healer, just a medtech."

"What's the difference?" she asked. He seemed perfectly competent as a doctor to her, no hesitation in his manner as he adjusted the machines around her.

The corners of his eyes crinkled with his smile, and he pulled a cage around her lower body. She still couldn't feel anything in her legs, and she knew she should feel *something* about that. Panic. Worry... anything. But she didn't. It was like her brain simply refused to recognize the fact she was paralyzed from the waist down.

"Latharian healers use a neural energy transfer system to connect directly with their patients," he explained. "They operate on their patients at the molecular level while keeping their systems operating and shouldering the pain load. It takes many years of training before they take their trials to become a full healer."

She blinked. "So they do everything... anesthetic, monitoring, and operating? All at the same time?"

"Exactly."

"Fuck... that's like..." She chuckled at her own thoughts. "For us that seems like magic right there."

Tal shrugged. "For a primitive society, any advanced technology would seem like magic."

"Hey! Are you calling me primitive?"

The medic winked, which earned him a growl from Zero. With a sigh, Tal looked up. "I'm not trying to steal your girl, big guy. We're just chatting before the procedure starts."

His expression dropped serious as he clicked the last part of the cage in place. "Unfortunately, I am not a full healer and can't take your pain load. So I'm going to have to rely on you to tell me when things get too rough and we'll up your pain meds. Okay?"

"Wait... what? Is this going to hurt Eris?" Zero demanded, surging forward again. Reaching out, she grabbed his hand before he could get past her.

"It's okay. Really," she told him. "If he thinks he can fix me... it's got to be worth a shot."

9

*Z*ero stomped into the cargo bay a few hours later with the distinct need to punch something. Several somethings. Several somethings *many* times.

Growling under his breath, he closed his eyes and clenched his fists until the feeling went away. He'd stuck it out in medbay as long as he could, but the sight of Eris in pain had flipped switches he didn't know he had. Even though he *knew* Talent was trying his best not to hurt her, each time she winced or suppressed a cry, he wanted to break the medic into itty-bitty little pieces. Then stomp on them.

"Hey, big guy... who pissed on your parade?"

He looked up to find Red, the Warborne's

engineer, on the other side of the cargo bay, looking at Eris's suit with a gleam in her eye.

"Talent's patching Eris up. I... she's hurt. I don't like her being hurt," he explained gruffly as he walked over, trying to shrug his anger off like a second skin.

Being snippy with Red was never wise. Not unless he wanted to spend the next few weeks with a temperamental shower unit in his quarters, or his lights permanently on disco. The rest of the crew had quickly learned what not to do from watching Fin, who regularly rubbed the half-Krynassis female the wrong way.

He was currently on week four of the food prep units deciding he liked his morning coffee "superchill" or "lava hot." In Zero's opinion, the tall Navarr was sweet on Red and did it on purpose to get a rise out of her. But he'd never say it within earshot of either of them. Sucking vacuum the wrong side of an airlock wasn't his idea of fun.

Red slid him a sideways glance, arms folded over her chest. She was a tall female, nearly the same height as he was, so she didn't have to crane her neck. "Huh. Yeah... Another one bites the dust."

He frowned. "What was that?"

"Nothing." She shrugged and then waved an electro-spanner at the suit. "Humans built this?"

"Yeah. Why?"

"Impressive."

Red wasn't effusive with praise. He'd expected a derisive comment, something about humanity being toddlers when it came to higher-level tech and space exploration, so the comment caught him off guard.

"Yeah?"

She nodded, her lips pursed as she considered the suit. It was upright now, and she'd already plugged it into a power module to charge. He winced at the damage it had taken. Some of the armoring had been torn loose and there were bullet holes everywhere. His blood ran cold as he realized just how close Eris had come. All to save him and Sparky.

"For saying the humans built it, yes. It's some advanced-level thinking right there. I mean, yeah... the execution is a little shoddy. Servos and wiring are rudimentary at best, but the *idea* of it?" Her lips quirked as she looked at him again. "It's nearly as impressive as you are, Toaster."

He groaned. "What will it take for you to forget that stupid nickname?"

She grinned, twirling her spanner. "How about

you help me fix up this little beauty for your girl? I'll bet she won't like seeing those holes in her."

"No. She really will not."

He stepped forward, eager to have something to do. For the next hour or so, he and Red crawled over the armored suit, mending panels and sorting out damaged wiring units. As always, he and Red worked in companionable silence. The comfortable rhythm soothed his soul.

Then Red sighed and dropped her wrench into her toolbox.

"Okay, big guy," she said, arms resting lightly on her knees as she sat on a gantry next to the suit's shoulders. "Out with it. What's bugging you?"

He looked up to find her studying him with a gaze as unblinking as a snake and twice as dangerous. Since she actually *did* have scales some of the time, the analogy was unerringly accurate. With a sigh, he put down the welding gun and faced her. It was pointless trying to argue with her. She'd just keep going until she got the answers she wanted.

"It's Eris," he said bluntly. "She's so delicate and beautiful. And I'm..."

He grimaced and waved a hand to indicate himself—from his crooked nose where it had been busted in a cage fight in some dingy bar he couldn't remember the name of through his metal arm to the implants under his skin. "I'm more metal and circuitry than man. How could she want someone like me? I'm just a machine."

The lack of self-confidence was new and totally unlike him, but he'd never met anyone like Eris before. Someone who made him think, made him *feel*... made him want to be better than he was.

From the moment he'd met her, he'd wanted her, and he just realized it was more than him wanting to get her into the sack. He wanted more from her than to get his hands on her gorgeous body. Although, he'd be lying if he tried to claim that wasn't a consideration. He wanted her as a person. And he wanted her to *like* him. Maybe more...

"You listen to me, Zero." Red's voice was firm as she dropped off the gantry to stand in front of him. "I've known you since T'Raal pulled you half-dead out of that gods-damn wreckage. You are *not* just a machine. If you think that, I'll happily go a couple of rounds in the ring with you and give you enough bruises to prove you're a living, breathing, *feeling* being. Okay?"

She hooked her hand into the back of his neck, bringing his forehead down to rest against hers.

"You're no more a machine than I am a cold-blooded lizard."

Then she sighed. "I'm not good with this emotional shit, but you are one of the best men I know. You're sensitive and caring, and I love you like a brother. Which means I have no problems putting the beat-down on you if you keep talking crap like this. Okay?"

His lips quirked. "So your way of dealing with my existential crisis is to threaten to kick my ass? You do see the irony in that, right? Your way of showing familial love is an expression of violence."

"*Affectionate* violence," she corrected. "And I promise not to kill you."

"Gee, thanks," he muttered hoarsely past the lump in his throat.

"You're welcome. Any of us would do the same. We're Warborne, remember? Warborne first. Warborne always."

"Warborne always."

The instant Zero got the notification from Talent that he was releasing Eris from Medbay, he put down his tools and practically ran through the corridors to get her. Since the *Sprite* was a small ship, that mainly resulted in him bouncing off several walls and almost flattening Skinny coming the other way. Since the heavy-worlder was a unit and a half no one wanted to take on in a fight, that was saying something.

"Hey! Where's the fire?" Skinny yelled as Zero passed him at a run.

"Sorrycan'tstopthanks!" Zero called over his shoulder, turning the corner and almost running right into Talent helping Eris walk through the medbay doors.

"Hey, beautiful! What are you doing on your feet?" he asked, scooping her up and glaring at Talent. The little human had just been severely injured, and Talent had her walking around?

"Hey." His ire disappeared. When she looked at him that way, her eyes all dark and soft, he struggled to focus on anything but her. "Talent just finished my treatment. I can actually feel my legs!"

"That's awesome."

He nuzzled her nose with his. He didn't care about the display of affection in front of his shipmate. Not with what Red had just said to him. "But should you be walking yet? Shouldn't you be resting up?"

"Actually, gentle movement is the best thing for her right now," Talent broke in, a knowing smile on his face as he leaned against the wall with his arms folded across his chest. "I had to repair a lot of her neural pathways and synapses, but they need sensory input to embed correctly."

He shrugged at Zero's curious look. "Had to do a lot of replacement calibration in the healer's hall. It's more engineering than healing, so they left it to me a lot of the time. Was *beneath* the healers..." The curl of his lip gave an indication of his feelings on imperial healers. "This was just the same but connecting nerves back to nerves rather than cybernetic constructs."

"Oh?" Eris asked, interest in her eyes as she looked between them. "So you've worked on people like Zero as well?"

Talent chuckled and shook his head. "No, they broke the mold with him. I worked on Latharian warriors who'd had cybernetic replacements. Now... if you're going to wrap her in cotton wool," he said to Zero, "at least make sure she gets up and uses the facilities herself. Even a slow walk around the primary deck corridors if she feels up to it. *Gentle* exercise is good."

"Got it, doc." Eris patted Zero's broad shoulders. "I'll make sure he takes me out someplace nice or something."

"I hear El Cantina at the rear of the ship is nice,"

Talent's lips quirked a little as he fell into the game. "Service is a bit *trall,* though. You have to cook your own meals, and the waiters are often rude. But it has a nice view of the .... Err... aft bulkhead. The reflection from the overhead lights is lovely in the evening."

"Can't wait," she smiled at him over Zero's shoulder as he turned and stomped away up the corridor. "Hey, I was still talking!"

"You need to rest," he told her gruffly, his expression tight. He wouldn't meet her gaze and barreled through the third door down the corridor. She winced as he caught his shoulder, feeling the impact even through his bigger body.

"Hey... slow down. It's okay. *I'm* okay," she reassured him, putting her hands on his cheeks and making him look at her. He still wouldn't look at her, his adam's apple bobbing. He sighed, closing his eyes and leaning into her touch.

"I hated it," he admitted. "You being in pain. I can walk through a hail of bullets and control a ship without touching it, but I couldn't help you. It tore me apart inside. I know we've not known each other long but... you're important to me, Eris. I can't explain it."

"Then don't," she whispered, moving her hand to

run her thumb lightly over his lips, tracing them. "Don't talk... don't analyze. Just *feel*. That's all we need. Just the two of us. Together. Okay?"

He nodded, the movement jerky.

"Together," he replied, his voice husky.

Walking across to the bed, he laid her down gently and then stood, running a hand through his short hair, which turned it into a mass of ruffled spikes. He looked critically at the bed.

"You might get cold. I should get you more blankets."

She laughed and grabbed his hand as he began to turn away. "I might... so you should get down here and warm me up. Shouldn't you?"

He didn't resist her, letting her pull him down. She sighed as she curled up in his lap, her head against his shoulder. It was hard to explain, but she felt better with him around. She felt safe, secure. After years of having to rely on herself rather than run the risk of having to return to her family, tail between her legs, it was nice to have someone. Even if it was an illusion.

She was more than familiar with the rush of battle and the closeness it could forge. She'd seen more than a few of her comrades fall for each other in the heat of battle, only for their marriages to fall apart in the cold light of a peacetime day. But for right now, she'd take the comfort, even if it was fleeting.

Silence stretched out between them. Comfortable, but charged. His hand swept up her arm, and her breathing caught, heart starting to thunder as the fine hairs rose in the wake of his touch. She tilted her head back as his hand cupped her nape, her entire body flooding with warmth at the dark heat in his eyes. His gaze flicked down to her lips. His tongue darted out to wet his lips and she almost groaned.

She wanted him. So badly she ached. She wanted him more than she'd ever wanted a guy in her entire life.

Surging forward, she kissed him, a shiver of pleasure bursting through her body at the first contact of their lips. Her hands weren't idle, spreading over his chest... every part of him she could touch as she tilted her head and deepened the kiss, the impatient aggressor as her need to claim him as her own rode her hard.

She got to keep control of the kiss for a few seconds. Then he growled in the back of his throat and turned her on the bed, pinning her beneath him even as he braced himself on his arms to keep his weight off her. His kiss was ruthlessly efficient, and she whimpered, the sound lost beneath his lips as she clung to him.

There was no more conversation. There was no need for words. Heat flared between them like a super nova. She gasped as he broke the kiss to pull her head back and kiss down her neck. His lips left a trail of fire that tingled over her skin and her body clenched in response. She tore at his shirt, needing to get it off him. Needing to touch him.

He pulled away for a second to yank his shirt up and over his head, and her higher brain functions short-circuited at the display of carved male muscle and satin skin. Taking advantage of his movement, she leaned up on her elbow to kiss his chest. His breath caught, the small sound the sexiest she'd ever heard. Until she slid her hand down the front of his body, cupping him through his pants, and he groaned.

"That's a sound I want to hear far more of," she whispered, flicking her tongue over his nipple. He flinched and hissed, his hand pushing hers out of the way to tear at his fly.

"Oh, you'll hear more of it. I promise," he rasped, his cock springing free.

She bit her lip as she wrapped her hand around

him and stroked. He was long and so thick she couldn't get her fingers to close all the way. That just sent a spike of anticipation through her so intense she almost whimpered again.

"*Fucking hell!*" he whispered explosively, his hand mangling the pillow by her head. He dropped his own head forward, eyes closed and expression taut as she learned the length and shape of him. She stroked and teased along his shaft before cupping his balls.

The soft movement broke the dam. He pulled back, yanking at her clothes.

"Naked," he ordered, voice clipped. "Now."

She grinned, shedding her shirt without a word. His eyes darkened as she snapped her bra off and dropped it to the floor. Normally she'd have wanted the lights off, but the dumbstruck expression on his face eased any reservations she had about her body. He looked at her like she was the sexiest woman in all of creation, which turned her on more.

Arching her back, she thrust her hands in her hair, sweeping it up as she posed for him and showed off her body. The cooler air of the room washed over her, raising the fine hairs on her skin, but the look in his eyes made her shiver.

He spat a harsh curse in a language she didn't

understand, his hands on her hips to strip her of her pants. They hit the deck a second later, along with her panties, but she didn't care. All she cared about was the heavily muscled guy parting her thighs with a rough shove of his knee. The roughness didn't bother her, not with the look in his eyes, somewhere between tortured need and unbridled desire.

Biting her lip, she locked gazes with him as he settled himself between her parted thighs, reaching between their bodies to set himself against her. A rush of heat escaped her as he slid the broad head of his cock between her pussy lips, brushing against her clit. He rolled his hips and she swore. With every rock, he stroked her clit, pushing her arousal higher.

She growled and hooked her hand around the back of his neck. "Zero, if you don't get inside me *right* now, I'll—"

Grinning, he leaned down and stole her words with a kiss.

"Gentle exercise, remember?" He broke away to whisper against her lips.

She lifted a leg to wrap it around the back of his hips. She didn't want to think about how easy the movement was or the fact that less than a few hours ago, she was facing down a life of... she cut the thought off before it could form.

"Gentle is good. Just... *now,*" she begged, trying to pull him closer.

His reply was to bear down. She gasped as he breached her. Her hands gripped his shoulders, fingertips finding purchase against skin and warm metal as he slid into her slowly. He filled her, parting her body widely around his thick shaft. She murmured in pleasure and delight. He was deliciously thick, rubbing against her in ways she'd forgotten existed. Her social life hadn't exactly been full these last few years.

"Now is also good," he rumbled, his lips brushing hers as he bottomed out. For a moment he held still, throbbing within her, but then he began to move. Slowly at first, watching her reactions as though he was scared of hurting her, but she saw... *felt* the control he was exerting over himself.

That care and control melted the last little reserve in her heart. But rather than complain and tell him he wasn't hurting her, she decided to show him instead. She kissed him and rolled her hips in demand. He gasped, rearing back a little to check her expression, but then his eyes darkened. His next thrust was harder. Faster.

They moved together, finding their pace and rhythm. Skin slid over skin, lips clinging as their tongues stroked and tangled. She felt every inch of him as he thrust into her, taking her over and over again. Claiming her as his. She arched into him, trusting to his strength as her curves fit against his harness perfectly.

But slow wasn't enough. She felt that as clearly as he did, urging him on silently. With a growl, he dropped down, caging her with his bigger body as he picked up the pace. And she was lost. Wrapping herself around him, she lost herself to the pleasure of touch and need. It built within her, an unstoppable storm of sensation and emotion.

It didn't take long for her to climb higher, hovering on the edge of ecstasy. She opened her eyes, wanting to see his face as she came.

"You're mine, Eris, for now and always," he whispered and he smiled tightly, cords in his neck standing out as he sped up.

The first harder thrust took her by surprise, the second took her to the edge of the abyss and the third threw her over it. She threw her head back and cried out, shattering apart in his arms. Pleasure coursed through her, rewriting her view of the world.

He grunted and slammed into her, each hard thrust sending new waves of ecstasy through her.

She watched him through half-lidded eyes as he thrust a last time, throwing his head back as he came with a growl. She felt it, the heat of his release as his cock jerked and pulsed deep within her. And she saw it, the pleasure on his face as he gasped and looked down at her.

Their gazes locked and amid their combined pleasure she felt their souls connect... Mesh...

Then become one.

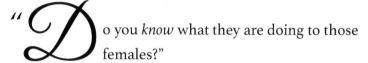

10

"*D*o you *know* what they are doing to those females?"

Talent burst out as he stormed onto the bridge. It was so unlike the usually unflappable medic that both Skinny and Fin turned in their station chairs in surprise. He stood in front of T'Raal in the captain's chair, practically bristling with rage, his eyes wild.

As always, T'Raal didn't bat an eyelid. Most males would be anxious to put some distance between themselves and the highly trained and very dangerous former imperial warrior, but he just looked up.

"Who? And what females?" he asked.

"The *humans!*" Tal broke away, shoving his hand through his hair as he paced the small briefing area at the back of the bridge. "They... what they did... *Draanthic!*"

Skinny turned fully to watch, concerned for his comrade. Since coming aboard, Talent had proven himself to be a capable warrior and ferocious in battle. Otherwise though, he was easygoing, so whatever the humans had done to rile him up so much, it must be severe.

"Calm down. Think and then speak," T'Raal ordered, his tone level as he rose from his chair, joining Talent at the back of the bridge. Folding his arms over a chest like a barrel, he watched the younger warrior in concern.

Tal took a deep breath, his expression tortured. "I've treated Zero's woman, Eris. Her wounds were not life-threatening but instead would have been life-altering. She sustained damage to her neural systems and without intervention would have been paralyzed from the waist down."

T'Raal's expression tightened for a moment, as did Skinny's. The idea of a female being injured in such a way was anathema to them. Even though they were Warborne, and not considered to be worth much to the "elite" of the empire, they were still Latharian through and through. Every female was precious and something to be protected. Apart from their own Red. Any attempt to protect the hard-as-nails half-breed female usually resulted in bruises.

"I'm assuming you managed to successfully treat her?" their leader asked.

Tal looked almost offended at the question and nodded sharply. "Yes. I fixed the damage and reconnected the pathways I could. She's with Zero now, with orders to rest and recover."

Skinny's eyebrow shot up toward his shaved hairline. Given how obsessed the big cyborg had been with the station chief since he'd first seen her a few weeks ago, he very much doubted the couple were resting right now.

"And you disagree with something the humans did?" Fin broke in, obviously just as curious as Skinny was. "Or do you simply object to their existence at this point?"

"That!" Tal pointed at Fin in agreement and started to seethe again. Visibly. Shit, whatever they'd done, it must be serious. "Those imbecile *draanthic* are performing surgery on females to put them in those suits. Adding implants to allow them to control the things."

Sitting at the comms console, with feeds from all over the ship, Skinny hadn't been able to resist taking a look at the feeds from the cargo bay where

Red was working. The human armored suit was something else. He'd never seen anything like it. It reminded him of the power armor the Warborne wore for space combat, but much bigger... like a cross between an imperial *drakeen* and combat armor.

The soldier in him wanted to take it for a whirl, especially with those big guns mounted on its shoulders. Still, even though he was no engineer, a glance at the open cockpit made him sigh. It was built for the tiny frames of humanity. He wouldn't even get his big toe in there.

"And this is a problem?" T'Raal was the voice of reason in the face of the enraged medic. That unflappable nature made him dangerous and had elevated the Warborne from simply a mercenary unit to *the* most famous mercenary unit in history.

"*Draanthing* right, it is! They put that shit in their bodies and they can't take that kind of load. Maybe a Lathar could, with the right enhancements, but a human? A human female? It's burning out their nervous systems and leaving them paralyzed!"

Skinny blinked.

"Wait... what? You mean Zero's woman wasn't an anomaly?" he demanded.

"*No!* That's my point!" Tal's outburst was loud

and filled with fury. "They're doing this *knowing* it's going to damage these females, and they don't care!"

Skinny's jaw dropped, no words making it past his lips. His astonishment and growing anger mirrored on both Fin and T'Raal's faces.

"But... why?" T'Raal demanded, the deepening of his voice evidence of his rage.

"Because they have so many females they don't care," Tal hissed. "They're seen as disposable."

"Fuck!" T'Raal exploded, his bellow of rage punctuated by a crash as his fist connected with the bulkhead by the bridge door. His knuckles came away scarlet, his chest heaving with anger as he looked at Tal.

Skinny and Fin half rose out of their chairs, everything else falling away as they watched their leader carefully. Waiting for his next move. They'd all seen him angry but never this furious. He'd always kept it together before. Always. So much so, Skinny had a side-bet with Fin that he had Izaean blood somewhere in his family tree and that one day he'd blood-rage out. It said a lot about the bat-shit crazy nature of the Warborne that they actually looked forward to the possibility of that happening.

Then he shook himself, like a *deearin* shaking water from its back.

"Find out how many and where," he ordered. "If they're going to do that to females, they don't fucking deserve them."

"*JESH!*"

Zero jerked awake, screaming again and convinced he was surrounded by fire and pain. His onboard argued with him as it gave constant readings on his surroundings, reassuring him his body temperature was normal and he wasn't sustaining the epidermal damage he thought he was.

But try as it might, his onboard couldn't get a foothold against the survival instincts screaming at him. The battling instincts, biological and cybernetic, kept him locked in place, his two halves vying for control. The glitch usually had him shorting out and already he felt his senses start to fade.

Then a soft hand landed on his shoulder, sliding around to his chest as a soft body pressed against his back.

"Hey," Eris murmured, her voice rough with sleep. "I got you. Don't worry."

He sighed, all the tension draining out of his body at her touch. It managed what his onboard could not, reassuring him that the dream was just a dream. He wasn't burning alive. He covered her hand with his, pressing it over his still-thundering heart as he closed his eyes and worked on calming down.

She was here. Everything would be alright. Everything *was* alright.

Her soft lips brushed against the side of his neck and she laid her head against his shoulder.

"I had nightmares when I first came out of the military," she said in a soft voice. "The accident that damaged my legs? It was in battle. I caught a grenade on my right leg. The armoring was substandard, parts made down to a price."

He rubbed his thumb over the back of her hand as she told her story, not interrupting her. Several times during their lovemaking she'd pushed his touch away from her scars. Especially a big starburst one on her hip. Instinct told him it was important not to push and just let her go at her own pace. She reminded him of C...

The thought slid away before he could grasp it. Normally he'd have been frustrated but now, with her here, it didn't matter. He was more interested in her story than his unreliable hide-and-seek memories.

"I couldn't move, so my unit left me to cover the rear while they took the objective," she carried on, and he registered the change in her voice. The tone was flatter, monotonous, as though she were merely an observer rather than a participant in the tale. "They walked into an ambush... somehow the enemy had shutdown codes for their suits. That wasn't even supposed to be possible. They were supposed to be on tight-ray modulation and uncrackable... but they did."

She shuddered as she leaned against him. "I had to listen as they were cut down, unable to move, unable to help them. In the end, I cut the motors free so I could drag myself to them... give some covering fire. But I was too late. They were already dead."

The deadness in her voice tore at his heart. "What happened then?" he asked softly.

"Medical evacuation. When I got back to base, the powers that be told me I had PTSD and hadn't heard it right. That I was making up stories because of survivor's guilt."

He growled in the back of his throat, but she shushed him up. "It's in the past."

Her lips brushed his shoulder again as she

cuddled closer. "So I know what it's like. I've been there. It's okay. You're safe."

The sigh punched free from his chest before he was aware it was there. Lifting her hand, he kissed her knuckles. "Thank you. For being here."

"Do you want to talk about it?" she asked softly, not moving from her position against him. He felt the soft curve of her breasts against his back and the steady beat of her heart. A sense of guilt hit him hard and fast.

"You're supposed to be resting," he argued, only to get a soft, sleepy chuckle in reply.

"We're just talking. Not much exertion in that. Is there? We had our gentle exercise earlier, remember?"

His lips curved, and he twisted quickly. A second later, she was in his lap, a soft squeak escaping her.

"The nightmare made me forget," he lied, gaze on her lips. "What gentle exercise was that?"

Her eyes darkened as she smiled up at him, lifting her lips for a kiss. "Oh dear. Memory problems. Perhaps I should call the doc…"

"I think all the treatment I need is right here," he murmured, lowering his head and claiming her lips for a long, slow kiss.

They didn't come up for air. The slow kiss exploded into torrid need and he turned them over, making her straddle him. They both gasped as he slid inside her again, and he spent the next few hours proving just how good a cyborg's memory was...

ZERO REALLY WAS the sexiest man she'd ever met.

Eris lay on her side, still warm and comfortable in a nest of the blankets on the bunk. They still held the warmth of his body and his scent, so she was in no hurry to leave them. Not when her view was so lovely as well.

Zero moved around the tiny cabin with the kind of grace some big men had, and it fascinated her.

"These rooms are tiny... for you guys I mean," she commented, watching him clean his teeth. The attached bathroom was so small he was half in and half out of it. If anything, it was smaller than her bathroom back on the station, and she hadn't thought that was possible.

"Can you even fit in the shower in there?" she asked when he looked over at her, eyebrow raised.

He removed the toothbrush to answer but the voice issuing over the ship-wide comm drowned him out.

"Miss. Archer, this is the bridge. We have an incoming message for you, from a... Mrs. Archer-Russell?"

She blinked in surprise, sitting up. "What? How the hell did she manage to get the message to me here?"

"It's not live, I'm afraid. We recovered your personal data stream from the last relay tower we passed by and picked up a couple of messages. I..." There was a pause and a cough. "Well, I figured you'd be a guest with us for a while, so I added your credentials to our comms array. I hope that was okay?"

"That's Skinny," Zero stage-whispered. "He's our comms guy. Ain't nothing he can't do with a radio."

There was a laugh from the speakers. "Yeah, it's a little more complicated than a 'radio' as you well know, Toaster. I'll send both messages through to your quarter's console."

"Thanks," Zero growled, disappearing for a moment to spit foam into the sink and rinse his mouth out. When he reappeared, Eris had wrapped herself in the lightest blanket and was sitting on the edge of the bed.

Movement this morning was far more comfortable than it had been last night, but she was still convinced she was in a dream. There was no way Talent could have fixed the totally fucking fubar that was her damaged nervous system all in one go. Could he?

"Toaster?" she asked as the big cyborg reappeared.

He grimaced. "Assholes, the lot of them. We were clearing out a possible Krin invasion on one of the *Velexian* system worlds when we passed an abandoned village. Skinny found a toaster... 'Hey, Zero, I found your mom!'"

Her eyes widened, and she slapped a hand over her mouth before she could laugh. "He *didn't!*"

"Asshole." Zero groused again, but she caught the quirk at the corner of his lips. "It was hilarious, but don't you dare tell him I said that. I've been fighting off them trying to change my nickname to Toaster ever since."

Her ears pricked up at that nugget of information. "So Zero actually isn't a nickname?"

He shook his head, sitting down at the chair in front of the desk bolted to the wall. He turned it around so he faced her, arms on his heavily muscled thighs. As she watched, the skin on his cheek under his left eye changed. Part of it became darker and then resolved into an alphanumeric code.

00-S1057

"What is that?"

His shoulder lifted in a nonchalant shrug. "No idea. Could be anything from a serial number to a comm number for customer services."

Zero zero... Shit. It *was* his name. Or the closest thing he had anyway.

Instantly she crossed the distance and was in his lap. His kiss tasted of toothpaste and clean man. She murmured under her breath in pleasure.

"Morning breath," she muttered, breaking away to hug him instead.

His arms wrapped around her, and she nestled closer to him. The fierce hug told her all she needed to know. About how much he needed the contact... and how much she did. Resting her head against his shoulder, she closed her eyes for a moment, savoring the closeness.

Then he shuddered and swept his hand down her back. "Okay, how about we look at these messages of yours, and then I can show you just how much room there is in my shower..."

"Men! You're bloody sex mad!" She laughed, mock slapping his shoulder even as he turned the chair so they both faced the screen.

"Nah... not a man, remember? I'm a machine... a *luuuurve* machine."

"Oh. My. God... Guys, did you hear thi—"

Zero groaned as the ship-wide comm cut off, his expression pained as he looked at her. "You do realize I will never, *never* live that down now?"

She chuckled, leaning over to kiss his cheek. "Yeah, well, it's accurate. Isn't it? I say own it. Now... how do I get my messages?"

With mingled foreboding and anticipation, she watched as Zero logged onto the system for her. The language on the screen was like nothing she'd ever seen before, although it seemed hauntingly familiar. Almost like she could squint, look at it out of the corner of her eye and it would resolve into something that would make sense to her.

"Latharian?" she guessed.

Zero nodded. "It's a common language for all of us. Most of the crew are either Lathar or half-Lathar. T'Raal and Talent are inner systems pretty boys, Skinny's a heavy-worlder, Beauty's backwater of some description and Fin's a Navarr. Red's half-Krynassis."

She shook her head in amazement. "And we thought we were alone out here."

"Yeah... right. In terms of space travel, you guys

are barely out the cradle." Zero snorted and then sat back. "Okay, all yours."

Somehow, amazingly, the screen cleared of alien writing, and she was looking at her inbox on the familiar Inter-sector communications system. There were two messages. One from her brother, and the other from her mother.

Oh shit. She'd forgotten about Eric's message. Having the most lethal special operations unit in the human systems shooting at you tended to do that. Reaching out to open it, she suddenly stopped her hand in mid-air.

"Crap. Will opening this let them track where we are?"

"Please... give us a little more credit than that," Zero chuckled. "Skinny will have bounced that off so many arrays they'll think you're in the Earth president's office."

Heat hit her cheeks.

"Dumb question," she muttered, but he kissed the side of her neck.

"Nah. Understandable. You're dealing with technology you're unfamiliar with. How would you know its limits and capabilities? It was a sound question."

She mumbled under her breath, but the heat on

her cheeks turned to a blush at the tone of approval in his voice. She'd never needed validation from any man, but... from Zero it made her feel all warm and fuzzy inside.

"Shit..." he said when she didn't reach for the screen right away. "Do you want to be alone to view them?"

"No... no, it's fine." She grabbed his hand when he made to move her out of his lap. "There's not going to be anything I don't want you to hear."

Tapping the screen, she opened Eric's message first. Rather than her brother's face as she expected, it was a notification from a message holding service that they had an encrypted data pack for her.

"Huh. Odd," she murmured. "We're heading to Praxis-Four. Aren't we? To pick up your other crew member?"

"Uh-huh." Zero had wrapped his arms around her, holding her close in a cuddle she was really rather enjoying. Settled in his lap like this, warm and comfortable, she could easily forget there was a bounty on her head. Or that, miraculously, alien medicine had repaired the damage to her legs. A long, slow shudder escaped her as something, the smallest feeling, expanded in the center of her chest. She hadn't wanted to believe it, in case it was a dream she'd wake up from, but... here and now, it sank in.

"You okay?" Zero asked softly as her head dropped back to his shoulder. Closing her eyes, she nodded, her throat too thick at present to speak. Without saying a word, he held her for a few minutes, letting her absorb her new reality.

Sitting up, she shook herself and reached for the screen again.

This time, she wasn't as lucky with the message. Her mother's angry face appeared on screen, and they both winced as Catherine Archer-Russell screeched.

"Eris! What the bloody hell do you think you're playing at? Getting a price on your head? Dealing with terrorists? Do you know how much trouble you're going to cause your father—"

"He's my fucking *step*father!" Eris hissed under her breath, even though the recording couldn't help her.

"You've disgraced the family, and if you think you're getting away with it, you've got another think coming!" Her mother wagged her finger at the screen like Eris was five years old. *"In fact, young lady, if you don't get your backside back to Earth to explain yourself to your*

father and me, there will be hell to pay, you mark my wor—"

"Yeah, so done with that already." Eris reached out and cut her mother off mid-screech. Looking over her shoulder, she caught Zero's eye. "I do believe someone mentioned something about breakfast?"

11

*E*ris hadn't seen much of the ship last night, just the medbay and his quarters, so her eyes were wide on the short walk to the galley.

"Whoa, I didn't realize how big this thing was," she said as he led her down the corridor, keeping a close eye on her until he was sure she was stable walking. The last thing he wanted to do was compromise her recovery. Not only because he didn't want Talent yelling at him, but also because he couldn't bear the thought of her in pain. Ever.

"It's actually a small warship," he explained, waving his hand over the door plate to the galley. It opened with a soft whoosh and she stepped past him. The delicate scent rising from her skin, the shower gel from his cabin and a smell that was uniquely hers, wrapped around him, holding him prisoner for a moment. Heat rolled lazily through his body, stirring a reaction south of the border he only just managed to stifle. Cyborg control for the win.

"Yeah... I meant that literally everything is bigger."

She waved at the tables and benches bolted to the walls and floor and he realized what she meant. The Lathar were built on a larger scale than humanity so she was tiny in comparison.

"Look, my feet don't even touch the floor." She chuckled when she sat down, swinging her legs. "I feel like a kid again."

He smiled and headed for the food prep counter, asking over his shoulder. "In that case, what do human kids like to eat for breakfast?"

"Usually anything that's as unhealthy as possible. Like... ice cream and pancakes?"

He paused for a moment and then a wicked little grin spread over his lips. "Pancakes I can do. Hang tight."

The door to the galley opened again, Tal and his little mate Lizzie, appearing in the doorway. Lizzie's face lit up when she spotted Eris, and she was through the door before Talent could take a step.

"Hey! You must be Eris," she said, plunking herself down opposite and extending her hand. "I'm Lizzie. Tal is my mate."

"Hey, Eris," Tal slid into the seat next to Lizzie. "How are you feeling this morning?"

"I'm good." She smiled. "No aches or pains. Whatever you did, it was definitely magic."

"Okay, good." The medic wrapped his arm around his mate, pulling her close. It was an entirely subconscious act, and Lizzie smiled up at him. "Take it easy for the next couple of days, and then all being well, I can sign you off as fit and healthy."

Zero listened in on the conversation as he prepared the mixture and set the plate to heat up. Hearing Eris chat away comfortably with his crewmates, the two human women talking ten to the dozen, eased some of the tension he'd been carrying. He wanted the rest of the crew to like Eris. If they did, and she liked them, hopefully he could persuade her to stay longer.

The thought made him pause for a moment, coffee pot in hand. When they'd first met, he hadn't had any plans other than wanting to get to know her, but things had gone way beyond that. He didn't want her to leave when this was all over.

Placing the coffeepot in the middle of the table,

he caught her eye. He smiled, reassured by the way her heart rate increased fractionally when she looked at him. Oh yeah, she was into him. She'd want to stay anyway. With him.

"Gods, what is that gorgeous smell?" Like they'd crawled out of the woodwork, more of the crew appeared in the doorway, Red looking at him in amazement with Skinny and T'Raal on her heels. Her gaze cut to Eris. "Girl, if you can get Zero to cook, you can stay!"

"Fuck off, Red! I cook!" Zero threw over his shoulder, pouring and flipping pancakes on the hotplate. At this rate, he'd need more than one batch of batter. "One of you lazy fuckers can lay the table if you're gonna gatecrash what was supposed to be a romantic breakfast."

"That would be me then," Fin quipped, following the others through the door and then easily moving around Zero in the tiny food prep area. Behind them, Red and Skinny had squashed onto one of the benches, watching him like a pair of *liraas* snakes for food. T'Raal took a seat next to Talent.

"Food's up. You gannets can wait," he ordered, slapping Red and Skinny's hands as they reached for pancakes. "Eris and Lizzie eat first. So behave."

They grumbled good-naturedly and sat back, waiting their turn. Zero waited by the table as Eris selected a pancake. Then he realized...

"Fuck! The ice cream."

The room went silent as he hit up the freezer unit, digging out a tub of his stash.

"*Fuuuuck me,*" Red whistled as he put it down in front of Eris. "It must be love. Zero never lets any of us anywhere near his triple-choc-caramel fudge."

Zero flipped her the bird, watching as Eris dug in. She popped a spoonful of pancake and ice cream into her mouth and then moaned.

"Oh my god, that is *so* good." She opened her eyes to smile up at him. "Where did you learn to cook like that? This is amazing."

"I'm glad you like it," he mumbled, a flush on his cheeks as he returned to the hotplate to work on the biggest stack of pancakes the *Sprite* had ever seen. He'd need to since everyone had decided to join them for breakfast. Soon the room was filled with the scrape of cutlery on plates and small sounds of pleasure.

"Pancakes? Did I miss pancakes?" Sparky appeared in the doorway, his dirty blond hair mused into bedhead spikes.

"Nope, you're just in time," Zero replied, sliding yet another plate loaded with a stack onto the table.

"Cool... smells good. Budge over, beautiful." He dropped into the seat next to Eris and grabbed a plate. Reaching for the top pancake, his fork clashed with Fin's both men looking up.

"Well hello, handsome. What's a nice guy like you doing in a place like this?" he quipped with a rakish grin.

Fin blinked, obviously not used to being hit on over breakfast, and pulled his fork back. "How do you know I'm a nice guy?"

Sparky claimed the pancake triumphantly. "Well, here's hoping."

"I got better shit to do than listen to this," Red growled.

She shoved her half-finished plate away and pushed herself to her feet. Before anyone could say anything, she was gone, the door sliding shut behind her. Without a pause, Skinny scooped her leftovers onto his plate. All was fair in love and food on the *Sprite*.

Taking advantage of the break in the conversation, Zero slid into the seat on the other side of Eris to eat his own breakfast.

"Woah, was it something I said?" Sparky looked all innocent, until Eris clipped him around the ear.

"Shut the fuck up and eat your food before these good folks decide you're an asshole and throw us off their ship," she ordered.

"Don't worry about it. I'm sure it's entirely Fin's fault. It usually is where Red is concerned." T'Raal chuckled, pushing his plate away with a sigh of contentment. "That was good. Thank you, Zero. Now..."

He focused on Eris. "Zero brought us up to speed. Any idea why your own people turned on you?"

Her plate finished, Eris cradled a mug of coffee in her delicate little hands and looked the large Warborne leader directly in the eye. "None whatsoever. I'm just an outer systems security chief, nothing special. They must have me mixed up with someone else."

"Do your people do that often?" T'Raal's question was valid, and one Zero very much wanted answered as well. But before Eris could answer, Sparky waved his fork.

"Nope. SO13 doesn't make mistakes like that. If they tried to kill you," he motioned toward Eris. "Then they *really* meant to kill you."

T'Raal looked between the two humans. "Who are SO13?"

"Special Operations Thirteen." Sparky scraped the last bits of syrup off his plate and licked the fork. "Highly secretive black ops unit. Professional killers basically. Ones that actually like killing. There's a rumor that they surgically remove all morals and your soul when you join the unit."

"Oh? How'd you know so much about them?" Fin demanded, leaning across the table. He hadn't taken his eyes off the tall human since he'd walked in the room.

"Yeah, Allen, how *do* you know so much about a special operations unit so secretive most people think they're a myth?" Eris asked pointedly.

"Was one. Then the assholes tried to kill me. It didn't take," he grinned. "So they threw me in Mirax. But, one thing I do know for sure. If they've got a target on your back, they absolutely will not stop until you're dead."

FULL AND HAPPY after Zero's excellent breakfast, Eris turned her attention to the next item on her internal to-do list. Her suit.

Citing the need for a little "alone time," she

quickly worked out where the cargo bay was. Since the *Sprite* only had three decks, it was a process of elimination that didn't take long at all. Like the rest of the ship, it was functional and utilitarian with bare metal walls and checker-pattern deck plates. Hard-wearing and easy to clean. Honest. Not pretending to be anything else.

But... it was also someone else's domain. Eris registered the other presence as soon as she stepped through the door and paused. She was just a guest on the ship, so the last thing she wanted to do was step on anyone's toes.

"Might as well come in if you're going to," a gruff voice announced from the upper level.

Jumping slightly, Eris twisted and looked up. Red, the second female member of the Warborne crew, was sitting on a catwalk against the back wall, a wiring panel open as she worked on its insides. A spaghetti mass of colored wires vomited from the gap, and the alien woman's long fingers worked quickly in the chaos.

"Hi. It's Red. Isn't it? I'm Eris Archer," she introduced herself as she located the nearest ladder to the upper catwalk. With its own lift and tilt mechanism, it could be maneuvered into place anywhere in the cargo bay.

"Yeah. Caught that." Red spared her a look as she reached the top of the ladder. Not one for conversation then. Eris cast about for something to say.

"I'm Red. But guess you caught that too." The alien woman's lips compressed as something sparked deep in the panel. "*Draanth it!* This wiring is fucking screwed."

"Anything I can help with?"

Red shook her head and gave a small grunt. "Almost done. Then I can show you what you came here for. 'Cause I'm pretty sure you didn't come down here just to introduce yourself again."

A flush warmed Eris's cheeks. "That obvious, huh?"

Red chuckled and then grimaced as she twisted something deep in the panel. "There, that should do it. It's that fucking idiot Fin's fault. The wiring in his quarters is on this loop, and it's dodgy. He's constantly overloading the fucker so I have to go in there and fix it."

Eris kept her mouth shut on that one. The way she'd reacted to Sparky hitting on Fin... yeah, there was history there for sure.

Red closed the panel, shoving her tools into belt loops. Her ship-suit was tied around her waist, the wifebeater vest she wore showing off muscular development Eris could only dream of.

"Looks like you work out a fair bit. Is there a gym on board as well?" she asked as they made their way down to the lower level. "Could do with testing out the patch job your medic did on my legs."

Red nodded. "Same corridor as the galley, carry on to the end. It's just a couple of storage spaces knocked through, but it's well equipped. Cardio machines, weights. Sparring mats. Just..." She looked Eris up and down. "If you're planning on dropping Zero on his ass, make sure to ping me. Okay?" She tapped her bracer-mounted wrist comp. "I'll record it."

Eris chuckled. "Yeah, right. You *do* know he's a cyborg? There's no way I'd be able to take him down. I'm only human. And female."

"Pffft... Then cheat."

Eris arched an eyebrow. She'd have pegged Red for straight down the line, must be better than men to be as good as men. "Isn't that...well, a little unfair?"

Red shrugged. "Then call it... adapt and overcome. It's not your fault that most males have in-built stupidity when it comes to females. Show a tear, and their protectiveness comes rushing to the fore. If all else fails, flash your boobs and that shuts down *all* their higher brain functions. That's when you double-tap them between the eyes."

Eris about choked. "I don't want to *shoot* Zero."

"Yeah, well... Obviously, don't do that on the *Sprite*," Red advised as she strode across the floor to the other side of the cargo bay. "Probably best you don't flash your boobs either unless it's at Zero. Not unless you want a blood bath on board."

"No! Definitely not!"

She might not know Zero too well just yet, but she knew enough to know he was the possessive type. Which was cute. On him. Not anyone else. She'd never wanted a guy to be all possessive over her before.

Then her attention was hijacked by the dust-sheet-covered form by the back wall. It was a familiar height and shape.

"Is that?"

"Uh-huh. Go ahead," Red motioned her forward. "She's a lovely bit of kit. It took me a while to figure out some of the systems but... color me impressed. You humans have some solid engineering kudos under your belt."

Eris reached out for the sheet, butterflies in her stomach as she pulled it clear. Now she was back on her feet, her attention, like any good soldier's, had turned to her equipment and weaponry. She might not be in the military anymore but that didn't make her any less of a soldier.

But... she forced back her wince as the sheet started to slide. She hadn't been kind to the old girl. It was old tech and hadn't seen action for well over a decade. There was no way she should have taken her into combat, and she wouldn't have if those SO13 assholes hadn't declared war on her.

The suit had dealt with it like a champ, though. She'd been just as smooth to pilot as Eris remembered, responsive as hell, but she'd taken a battering. The armoring Eris had used to replace what was missing hadn't been the heavy-duty level that was on it originally, so she'd taken hits. Too many. The damage reports on her visual display when she'd finally made it to the *Aegis* airlock had been damning.

The sheet hit the floor and she slowly lifted her gaze, bracing herself for the sight of all the damage. But instead of the bullet-holed panels and busted servos she'd expected, the suit gleamed. Her panels were straight and true, though not unmarked. She could see where repairs had been made, the bullet holes still decorating the suit's hide, but they'd been filled somehow.

"What the..." she breathed, reaching out to run her hand over the metal skin. It was smooth. She couldn't feel the difference between the old metal and the new. Her gaze clashed with Red's in curiosity.

"We got a few tricks up our sleeves humans don't. We got all the internal and external damage fixed. And gave her an extra layer of armor." She tapped one of the filled bullet holes.

"Nano-molecular tri-chromidium," the alien engineer said as if that should mean something to Eris.

"The who what now?"

Red gave an apologetic grin. "Sorry, forgot most people don't speak engineering nerd. Basically, your suit now has a thin layer of stretchy metal armor as well. If it takes a hit, the nanolayer registers the shock of the impact and reinforces itself at that point for a millisecond. It flows to where it's needed and then resets itself. Kind of like when you punch sand, it hardens for a moment?"

Eris nodded. She'd never been near sand nor felt any desire to punch it, but the explanation made sense.

"Thank you *so* much. You have no idea how much this means to me. So... when can I take her for a test drive?" she asked, itching to get behind the "wheel" again.

Red chuckled. "You sound like you're Warborne born and bred. As soon as Tal signs you off, she's all yours. Promise."

THE TRADE OUTPOST on Praxis-Four was quite possibly the shittiest location Eris had ever seen. And that was with a career filled with being stationed in shitty places. Hell, she'd even take the ice-moons in the Trinaxis system over this place, which was saying something.

Praxis-Four was a desert planet, but not the nice type filled with picturesque golden sand dunes and sparkling oases. No, it had the honey-badger version of sand. Sand that got all up into everyone's nooks and crannies and totally didn't give a shit. It was the kind of sand that only needed a little encouragement and a slight breeze to shot-blast flesh from bones. Which was the reason she and the rest of the Warborne landing party had every square inch of skin covered.

Each of them wore a heavy coat over their ship

suits, which, she was amused to discover, bore the logo of an outer system gas haulage company. Pant legs were tucked into boots and sleeves into gauntlets to cut down any access the sand might find on the walk from where they'd hidden the shuttle out in the dunes to the outpost. Scarves and goggles covered their heads and eyes, all their features hidden. They blended in with the other inhabitants of the outpost, and she breathed a sigh of relief. She'd been worried she'd be spotted and recognized from the wanted announcements, or that the Warborne would be identified as aliens.

She needn't have worried. No one gave them a second glance as they walked along the main street. Well, nothing more than was normal for a hauler crew from out of the system anyway. They attracted the usual level of attention. Eyes watched them from the shadows and shielded doorways, assessing whether they could be lured down a side alley and relieved of whatever valuables they were carrying.

That interest waned when Skinny and Zero brushed aside their outer coats, revealing heavily loaded weapons belts. Suddenly they became less interesting than the sand that swirled and danced around their ankles as they headed for the central plaza of the outpost.

"Anyone have a bead on the hole Beauty's likely to have disappeared down?" Skinny asked over comms, his voice deep and rich in her ear. His tone and inflection were almost spot-on for Terran. During casual conversation she wouldn't have picked up he was an alien, but the more she listened to the Warborne talk between themselves, the more she picked up the odd inflections and phrasing that marked them as non-Terran speakers.

Except Zero. His speech patterns were entirely human. It must be because of his cybernetics. He'd only told her a little about his internal systems, but if half of what he'd said was true, he wouldn't have any problem picking up languages.

"He said something about checking out the market," Red replied. "Something about getting some Terran history books or something."

There was a collective groan from the others.

"Again?" Skinny shook his head. "He'll have to sleep on the damn things soon."

"He can download books from the communal servers," Eris commented. "If it's *real* books he's after... yeah, he might get something from the flea market. There's usually one in places like this."

Skinny turned. Even though his face was covered, the horror was evident in his voice. "Terrans sell *fleas?* Seriously... what is *wrong* with you people?"

She couldn't help the smile that spread across her face, hidden by her scarf. "Are you kidding me? There's a big market for them."

"Right on," Sparky joined the fun, a glint in his eyes behind his goggles. "Pedigree bloodlines and all sorts. A good flea will cost you your left bollock and then some. Breeding tips are passed down through generations."

"Fleas..." Skinny shook his head again, only to have T'Raal punch him lightly in the arm.

"They're teasing you, you dumbfuck," he chuckled and then turned to check. "You *are* teasing. Aren't you?"

"Yeah, we're teasing."

"Awww fuckit," Sparky grumbled. "We could have kept that going for hours!"

"Really, you all make it too fucking easy," she laughed, enjoying the moment. It had been too long since she'd had this kind of camaraderie... fifteen years. Her humor faded and she nodded toward the comms tower. "I'm going to need to head there to pick up my message. Catch you all at the flea market?"

"I'll come with you." Zero moved to her side

instantly, his tone firm. She didn't argue. It would be kind of nice to have someone to watch her back for a change. Especially in a place like this.

"Cool," T'Raal nodded. "Stay alert and on comms. Any problems, shout... *lurve machine.*"

Zero flipped him the bird and the three Warborne ambled off with Sparky, still laughing, in the direction of the flea market.

Despite their casual act, she noted the aliens still moved as a team, aware of each other and their surroundings as well as the human in their midst. It was easy to see they had military training, but nothing about them or the way they moved pinged her senses—either those from her former life as a soldier or her current one as a security chief.

Correction, *former* security chief, and now wanted criminal and suspected terrorist.

Shit, that was going to take some getting used to...

12

"Let's get going." Zero nudged her arm and they started walking.

It didn't take them long to reach the comms tower, just a few minutes' walk, but by the time they'd reached it, all her senses were on high alert. Unfriendly eyes watched them. She just hadn't worked out yet if it was the kind of unfriendly that would start shooting at them. If so, the new alien laser-blasters strapped to her hips were a reassuring weight. Even if they weren't actually laser-blasters. Zero and the other Warborne had rolled their eyes when she'd insisted on calling them that. And she'd joined them, ignoring Sparky making pew-pew-pew sounds back in the ship's airlock.

She slid her arm through Zero's, cuddling up close as though they were a couple. Well, she guessed they were, really, but that wasn't why she'd suddenly gotten all touchy-feely. He smiled down at her, the pleasure in his expression genuine, but she spotted the awareness there anyway.

"We're being followed," she murmured under her breath, smiling up at him as he held the door to the comms-tower office open for her. Pantomiming a curtsy, she swept inside like some gracious old-world lady, but she made sure to scan the room circumspectly in the same movement.

"Roger that," he replied, his voice relayed by the comms unit hidden in her ear. It felt low, intimate and she winked at him over her shoulder. He followed her through the door at a slower pace, a mock-leer on his face as he ogled her ass. She laughed and headed for the clerk's desk, stripping off her goggles, scarf and gloves as she went.

The office was the same as thousands of stream offices the galaxy over. Office beige panels covered the walls, the fake potted plants painted on in an attempt to create a calm and productive environment. The floor was plasti-concrete, a track of ingrained dirt leading her right to the clerk's desk.

Like the call booths lining the walls, it was bolted to the floor. Rough neighborhood then.

"Hey there!" she said brightly.

The clerk looked up. His expression—somewhere between bored, and "when does my shift end?"—didn't change as he looked at her.

"Welcome to K-Comms streaming. How can I help you today?"

The greeting was delivered in a dull monotone until the last word, which had a lilting up tone as out of place as a high society debutante in a marine barracks.

She gave him a winning smile. It was best never to piss off people like this. If you did, a routine thing like redeeming a message could become an hour-long task. "I'm here to collect a message? Message code—"

"Name?"

She blinked. Okay, that wasn't normal. She'd expected to input her code and a grunt as he waved her toward a booth. Normally these people wanted as little to do with you as possible. You were lucky if you got anything past the required company greeting.

"I have a redemption code?"

"*Yeaaaah*," the clerk clicked the top of his pen a couple of times. Rapid-fire. His expression didn't change, but the movement said everything she needed to know about his unusual request. Someone was paying him on the side. Had to be. "I'm gonna need your name. New rules."

"Kasra Emerton."

He frowned. "Kasra?"

"Uh-huh." She gave him an innocent, wide-eyed expression. Two could play games. "Name I was born with."

She sighed, thrusting her hip out and pouting as she studied her nails. "Now d'ya want this collection code or not? Cause my ship's gonna be putting in at Centaris in a couple of weeks, so I can just hit up the stream tower there..."

She let the sentence trail off, watching his expression out of the corner of her eye. Comm relay companies only got paid on collection, so if she went with a rival service, he'd lose the commission on the message. And in a place like this, every script counted. The question was, was that commission worth more than whatever he was being paid to find out her name? Or would he go for both...

"No..." he caved with a sigh. "No, that won't be necessary. Redemption code?"

She tried not to give him a smug smile. Probably failed. Made no difference either way. A couple of minutes and they were out of here. "Sierra-seven-three-four-nine-echo."

He tapped the code into the screen in front of him and then nodded toward the booths. The light above one of them turned green.

"You're in four."

She nodded her thanks, ambling that way. Zero leaned against the wall by the door. He gave the tiniest nod. Given his... unique abilities, she was sure he was monitoring the street outside. Good, at least she had a little time to recover this message.

Opening the door into the booth, she avoided the gaze of the guy in the next cubicle. Leaning against the glass, he was obviously hooked into one of the porn-streaming services, his shoulder shaking from the action of his hand behind the screen. He leered at her, so she slapped the privacy button, and the glass frosted.

"Asshole," she muttered to herself as she faced the screen. Words scrolled over the screen in green.

Message redemption in progress. Identification code: Sierra-seven-three-four-nine-echo.   Please   enter confirmation sequence.

Her hands raced over the keyboard as she keyed

in the code she'd memorized. The keys were sticky. She tried like hell not to think why, especially with the current activities of her neighbor in the next booth... Suddenly she wished she'd left her gloves on. She'd need to bleach her hands when they got back to the ship.

"Come on, come on..." she muttered under her breath, watching as the logo on the screen circled. And circled. And circled.

The longer it took, the more her shoulders tightened. Something was wrong. It shouldn't be taking so long. Perhaps the clerk hadn't been paid to find out her name, but to keep her here long enough to call for backup.

The hairs on the back of her neck stood up. Like... SO13 backup.

The door to the booth behind her was yanked open, making her squeal softly in surprise. Zero filled the frame, expression grim.

"We've got company. We need to move *now*."

Before she could answer, the console behind her bleeped. She yanked her gaze from Zero's back to the screen.

Message downloaded. Thank you for your business.

"Done," she replied, yanking the data-strip from

the port. It glowed green at one end to indicate a successful transfer. She shoved it into her pocket. She'd have to listen to it later... when they weren't in imminent danger.

"What's going on?" she whispered to Zero as he hustled her across the room toward the door. She didn't look but she felt the clerk's eyes on her all the way.

"The rest of the cre—" He didn't need to finish the sentence. The sound of a firefight back the way they'd come made both their heads snap around, one particularly loud and very human voice bellowing obscenities.

"Fucking hell!" Zero hissed, as they both took off at a run. "I swear I'm going to *fucking* throttle that bloody human."

THE FLEA MARKET, much to Skinny's disappointment, had nothing to do with fleas after all. Even though both the humans had assured him they were in fact joking and they didn't actually breed fleas, he'd still held out hope for something... anything... exotic.

But no. The back-street market on Praxis-Four

was just the same as every grotty back-street market in the ass-end of any system. They all had them, those places on the fringes of existence where the desperate and the morally corrupt congregated. Some days it was hard to tell which was which.

"Anyone gets eyes on Beauty, yell," T'Raal ordered, motioning for them to split up. His grim demeanor was a reminder that they didn't need to watch their asses. They were all well aware that technically they were operating behind "enemy" lines. Most of them were Lathar of some kind, even Red... though no one reminded her that without either a large amount of alcohol and liquid courage in their system, or a foolproof escape plan... and the empire in its infinite wisdom had banned any incursion into Terran space. Yeah... they were breaking all kind of rules on both sides of the fence even being here.

Skinny rolled his shoulders as he moved off toward the north sector of the market, making sure his heavy jacket sat loosely on his shoulders. He needed easy access to his weapons. Praxis-Four was Terran, but he knew better than to discount any of them as a threat. Humans could be just as mean as any Lathar, and given the right encouragement or enough alcohol, they'd take on fights they knew they couldn't win.

Just... because.

"D'ya think you'll need them guns, squire... or will your withering gaze decimate your enemies instead?" a mocking voice sounded at his side.

Skinny bit back a sigh. Sparky. Just his luck, the lone human had decided to latch on to him.

"Just staying loose," he replied, turning and sweeping a gaze around. Stalls were crammed in cheek to cheek, and each of the vendors tried to yell over their competitors.

"Penny 'ah pound, get yer fresh vat-grown veggies 'ere!"

"'Gi Sausages! The best pseudo-protein on the planet!"

"Iso-taurine drops! Keep them levels up!"

He drowned the noise out and focused instead on searching the crowds for the familiar form of their missing crew member. Well... not technically missing since they knew Beauty was here somewhere. He also had a habit of doing this, going on walkabouts. The quietest member of the mercenary team, none of them really knew that much about him. Not that they needed to. Like the rest of them, he'd been brought into the Warborne by T'Raal.

Apparently, he'd been a fighter in the combat pits in the hellholes of *Tarviisa*. The place was a cesspit where flesh of any kind could be bought, whether that be for fighting, fucking, or killing. There were no rules on *Tarviisa*. Even imperial warriors didn't linger long lest they find themselves on the wrong side of those pit barriers.

According to T'Raal, Beauty had fought in the pits for over five years. Skinny shuddered. After living through a nightmare like that, the guy could be forgiven for being a little on the quiet side and preferring the company of his books.

Books.

"Hey," Skinny slid a glance at Sparky. "Where would you get books in a place like this?"

"Huh?" Sparky struggled to tear his attention away from something, and Skinny sidestepped to see what he was looking at. Only to spot Red bent over as she checked out some mechanical do-dad that had caught her eye a couple of stalls down.

Skinny gave a low whistle. "Yeah... that there's a road to bruises and broken bones, my friend. If Red wants you, believe me, she'll let you know."

"Yeah?" Sparky cut him a sharp look. "You ever done her?"

There was real jealousy behind the tone. Skinny laughed and backed up, hands in the air. "Gods no, she'd eat me alive. *Oh, I'm so sorry—*"

He broke off as he was jostled from behind. Spinning around to apologize, his words trailed off as he found himself looking into the brightest pair of amber eyes he'd ever seen. Their owner was a tiny human female, masses of dark hair piled on top of her head in an elaborate hairdo that he instantly wanted to ruin by shoving his hands through it.

"No, no..." She smiled, and he was lost, reduced to speechless wonder at the heavenly symphony of her voice. "Totally my fault," her voice rose a little and she lifted a hand, halting the motion of the two men with her toward him. Belatedly he realized they must be her bodyguards. "Please, accept my apologies. Mr..."

"Errrr... Altav," he answered, surprised enough to give his real name.

She smiled and he got it together enough to notice she was dressed far better than most of the other market-goers. The dress that swathed her curvy figure looked expensive and the jewels around her neck... he was surprised she managed to walk around a place like this unmolested. A fortune like that would have even the most law-abiding citizens here working out how quickly they could part her from her jewels and dispose of her body.

"A pleasure to meet you, Altav." She held out her hand with a smile, shaking her head as one of the bodyguards gave a small growl.

Before he could take her delicate little hand though, Sparky shoulder-barged him aside. "A pleasure to meet you as well, Miss Ingrassia. But I'm afraid we really have to be going, our ship is about..." He shoulder-barged Skinny again. "To leave without us. Come on, big man. You know how pissy the boss gets if we're late."

"Of course," Miss Ingrassia smiled politely, folding her hands elegantly in front of her as Sparky all but dragged him away. Skinny managed to get a look over his shoulder, meeting her gaze one last time before the crowds shifted like sand and swallowed her up again.

"What the *fuck* was that all about?" he hissed, turning on the human. "She was fucking *gorgeous.*"

"Yeah." Sparky's expression held none of its normal jokiness. "Gorgeous and fucking deadly. That there was the poison princess, daughter of *the* most brutal asshole in this sector. This place," he motioned above his head to indicate the planet and systems around them, "is run by a group of 'elected' premiers. The Ingrassias are among the worst of them. Believe me, you do *not* want to fuck with them, especially that one. If her daddy found out you'd defiled his precious little flower, he'd reach down your throat to rip your cock and balls off and then feed them back to you. That's if little miss butter wouldn't melt in her mouth didn't poison you first. Her daddy's tried to marry her off three times so far. Each time, the groom never makes it to the wedding night."

"Shit."

"Yeah."

Skinny looked back the way they'd come but there was no sign of the beautiful Miss. Ingrassia. Which was probably a good thing. He'd never had such a reaction to a woman before.

"So," Sparky said brightly. "Books are this way. Let's find your boy and get the fuck off this planet."

It didn't take them long to find Beauty. Sparky wove his way through the stalls like he'd lived on this backwater dustball all his life until they reached the back wall of the market. There, to his amazement, was a stall with actual books. And, pouring over them, was Beauty, his expression rapt as he looked along the decaying spines of the obsolete objects.

"Hey, handsome," Sparky sidled up. "Looking for anything specific?"

Skinny sighed. Sparky really would hit on anything. Wouldn't he?

"Ignore him, Beaut. You got everything you need?" he asked, saving the human from a kicking. Beauty might be the quiet type, but he didn't like people invading his personal space without warning.

"Yeah, I'm good." Beauty nodded, showing Skinny an armful of books. Quickly he paid the vendor with human currency. Skinny wondered briefly where he'd gotten it, but with Beauty, it was best not to ask.

"I see you couldn't shake the human yet," Beauty gestured toward Sparky as they turned and made their way to the front of the market. Skinny had informed the others by way of a triple tap on the side of his neck where his sub-dermal comms were implanted. By now they should all be making their way toward the front of the market so they could all head back to the ship.

"Oi! Stop! Yeah, you!"

A shout behind them made Skinny frown and turn. One of the bodyguards that had been with

Miss. Ingrassia barreled toward them, bulldozing people out of the way and waving his gun around.

"Awww shit," Sparky groaned. "This is gonna get ugly fast. *Run!*"

And that was when the whole marketplace started shooting.

*Z*ero and Eris sprinted down the road toward the chaos and gunfire. Concern for his team warred with fear for the tiny woman running next to him, but she'd already more than proven herself in battle. He just wished she had her suit here. He'd feel far more confident not only with the backup of what amounted to a tank on legs but also because Eris would be safely wrapped up in a metal skin. He'd studied the schematics just as much as Red had while they were mending it, and with the improvements Red had made... yeah, you'd need a bunker buster just to put a scratch on its panels now.

It was a pity they were too far away for him to get an uplink with the ship and bring it here on remote.

He checked as they ran, just in case. Yeah. Fuck. Too far away.

He doubled down, increasing speed even as he kept an eye out around them. He'd picked up chatter on the local security services comm channel about an issue at the market, but that didn't mean there weren't other dangers out there. Eris had a bounty on her head and he was sure the shifty-looking clerk at the comms office had informed someone about their arrival. Dammit, he should have done a search on the origin of that message she'd picked up. Yeah, sure, it said it was from her brother, but digital IDs could be faked... hell, even comm-vids could be faked. Between them, he and Skinny could cook something up that had the emperor admitting on screen that his favorite color was pink and he wanted to give it all up to go hug trees in the outer systems.

They *could...* and it was tempting. But since he was sure the emperor would personally track him down and show him what his intestines looked like, he hadn't. He liked his innies to stay being innies, thank you very much.

Before they got halfway toward the turn to the flea market, the rest of the Warborne spilled out onto the main concourse, firing back at what seemed like the entire population of the outpost.

"Okay, who pissed off the locals?" Zero grinned as they caught up with the rest of the group. He and Eris slid into cover next to Red, who grunted.

"Skinny hit on the wrong local and now they're all trying to kill us."

Zero's eyebrow shot up. Skinny would not have been his pick for dangerous flirting. Sparky... it was practically expected, but not the strong, silent type heavy-worlder. Then they all ducked as the air around them became a deadly net of shrapnel and laser beams.

"You wankers!" a voice bellowed from the other side of the road, and Beauty ducked out of cover to fire back the way they'd come. His face was a mask of rage, one arm curled protectively around the books he carried. One of them had a hole and scorch-mark from a blaster on the back. "*That was a fucking first edition!*"

Three bodies hit the ground.

"It was *signed!*"

Two more bodies hit the ground.

"I'd say we leave Beauty to deal with the rest, but there are more on the way," Zero yelled in warning.

Seriously, he'd never seen the tactical specialist so pissed off. Ever.

"Moving!" T'Raal yelled and half the Warborne broke from cover as the remainder laid down covering fire. Zero's world narrowed down to firing arcs and making sure Eris was okay. He didn't give a rat's ass about his own skin, as long as she was okay. Despite the implants that laced her system, making her more like him than any of the others, she was still organic. Soft. Vulnerable.

He wasn't. His body was built for combat, his skeleton more a chassis than a biological construct, and his sub-dermal mesh was rated for ballistics. At least, it was now after Red had fired a full clip into his gut to test her theory. He still thought she'd enjoyed that a little too much.

"Keep it together," T'Raal ordered as they reached the edge of the outpost.

Crammed in beside Eris behind a small tumble-down wall, Zero scanned their surroundings. This was where it got interesting. They'd parked the *Sprite* out of town, a couple of sand dunes away. It had seemed like a good idea at the time. Now though, it meant they had at least a couple of hundred meters of blasting sand and tumbleweeds between them and the nearest rise. And absolutely nothing to stop their pursuers from filling them all full of holes.

"*Defensive line!*" T'Raal ordered from his cover behind a waste canister. It was amazing how such a big guy could fold himself into such a small space, but needs must when the bullets were flying. He motioned toward the sand behind them. "Zero and Red. We'll cover, you make it to the rise."

It made sense. Of them all, he and Red were the fastest on their feet.

"No can do, boss." It was the first time he'd ever argued with a direct order. "I'm not leaving Eris."

She looked at him like he'd grown another head. "What the fuck?" she hissed. "Do it and get us some covering fire, you idiot!"

Red barked a laugh. "I like her already. Okay, *lurve machine...* bet I can beat you to that top rise."

"The fuck you can!"

He caught Eris's chin and made her look at him. Her gaze was steady and unwavering. "Don't get shot," he told her. "Because if you do, I will be pissed with you. Okay?"

Then he kissed her. Quick. Hard. Barely more than an impression of lips on lips before he broke away.

"Okay, Scales... you're on," he called out to Red,

getting an outraged hiss in reply. She hated to be reminded of her Krynassis heritage. Even though it was written in the scales that appeared under her skin when she was stressed and this hiss sometimes in her voice.

"You lot had better put down covering fire," the female mercenary yelled a warning. "Because if this lot kill me, I will fucking haunt you all. Zero, moving in three... two... one... *go*!"

They both broke from cover at the same time, sprinting toward the top of the rise as the Warborne opened fire. Zero kept his head down, changing direction often as bullets and laser beams cut the air around him and slammed into the sand. About twenty feet away Red was going through the same song and dance, bellowing a wordless war cry.

They both made it to the top at the same time, throwing themselves into cover. But there was no time to rest and recuperate. Instantly, they clawed their way back up to the top of the rise, yanking weapons from holsters. Together, they opened fire on the outposters trying to ease from cover and overwhelm their friends still hidden on the edge of town.

Zero aimed, one of the townsfolk in his sights, and pulled the trigger. Bullets tore into the buildings, punching holes through walls and sending bodies flying. Blood sprayed scarlet to be soaked up by the ever-thirsty sand. The wind howled in triumph...

He frowned and pulled his finger off the trigger. His personal weapons were heavy-duty, sure, but they didn't pack that kind of punch... He and Red looked up as the wind whipped sand up around them, the ventral hull of the *Sprite* blotting out the sun.

"Anyone call for a ride?" Fin's voice boomed from the speakers as the *Sprite*'s forward guns cut down anyone trying to follow the team as they broke from cover and raced up the rise toward the ship. Zero grinned, waiting for Eris as she ran toward him and then bundling her up the boarding ramp ahead of him.

"So..." he yelled over the sound of the engine and the *Sprite*'s guns. "What did you think of your first action with the Warborne?"

ERIS WATCHED the boarding ramp shut behind them, the massive metal jaws swallowing them like a mama crocodile keeping her babies safe. Her ears still rang from the gunfire and her own heartbeat.

She slumped against the wall next to Zero as the ship lurched, g-forces making her unsteady on her feet for a moment as they took off.

"Hold on," Fin's voice came over the inter-ship comm, the words muffled. "Got turbulence in the upper atmosphere. Gonna be a little rough."

She grabbed a support strut at the same time everyone else made a grab for a handhold. Going for a burn when not strapped in was not fun.

The next few minutes were hell. The ship rattled and shook around them, and she seriously hoped the boarding ramp held. Zero had rolled over, his body half over hers as he pinned her in place against the bulkhead. She didn't argue. The warmth of his larger body was a comfort as she rested her forehead against his shoulder. And if a cyborg couldn't hold on, what hope did she have?

Her hearing had just about returned to normal when they hit space. The ship stopped shaking and everyone straightened up, letting go of whatever they'd grabbed to look at each other.

"So... what the hell happened there?" T'Raal growled, looking at Skinny and Sparky. Eris wasn't surprised that the former con was involved somehow. He always managed to find himself at the center of any shit that was going down.

Skinny shrugged. "Not a clue, boss. Bumped into a woman and apologized. I think her guards took exception because after we found Beauty, they started shooting at us, and it all went to shit."

T'Raal grumbled in the back of his throat as they all filed out of the loading bay. He shot a look at Sparky. "That what happened?"

Sparky nodded. "Honest gods truth, boss. He didn't even ogle her. She was probably jealous 'cause he left with me though. The ladies do love a bit of spark."

Eris sighed and looked away as his words were accompanied by a hip thrust she really didn't want burned into her retinas.

T'Raal turned his attention to her and Zero. "You guys get what you needed?"

She smiled, rooting the message strip from her pocket. "Easy as taking candy from a baby."

Beauty blinked, looking up. "You take candy from babies?"

She sighed. Lathar were so literal at times.

"They don't. It's just a saying. Means we had no problems," Zero said before she could and then took the message strip from her fingers.

She was about to complain, reaching to take it

back, when he said, "But I do want to check this before you play it. Just in case..."

Huh. That made sense. She'd already put him in danger once and look what had happened. SO13 had chased them through an asteroid belt. She didn't want to put the rest of the Warborne in danger. That would be a terrible way to pay them back for everything they'd done for her.

"Okay. We'll put it down to homicidal humans—"

"Hey!" Sparky protested. "I resemble that remark!"

T'Raal sighed, ignoring him as he continued talking. "—we'll put it down to homicidal locals. Put Praxis-Four down on the no-go list... and would someone please get that bloody shuttle back up from the surface! I don't want to leave anything for the locals to use to kill someone else."

The group went their separate ways down the corridors, Zero and Eris heading, not for his quarters as she expected, but to the lower deck. They passed the cargo bay and another door. The sound of raised voices emanated from inside, both male and female. Zero grunted.

"Engine core. That'll be Fin and Red. They have

a thing not-thing going," he said as they walked past. "They argue a lot."

"Ah... yeah, I thought that might be the case. Where are we going?"

"Computer core."

He stopped by a door just as it opened and motioned her to go ahead of him. She blinked as she stepped into the room, having to duck her head. With a low ceiling and metal walls, it was less of a computer core and more a computer closet. A single console was set into the wall over a metal desk bolted to the wall. One seat swung out from the wall and folded down. It was the sparsest, most utilitarian space and she turned. Yeah, a cleaning cabinet occupied the area behind the door. All in all, she'd seen more impressive coffee machines.

"This is it?" She motioned to the console on the wall. "I assumed it would be bigger."

He raised an eyebrow and then smiled.

"*That...*" he motioned to the screen, "is just the access point. Technically... all *this* is the core." He waved his hands around them. "We're sitting in the middle of it."

She blinked and put her hand out to place it against the wall. A soft hum prickled against her palm, working its way up her arm like a gentle welcome.

"Say hello to the *Sprite*." Zero smiled. "She's a *Tlerian-Seven* enhanced computer core. Capable of running an imperial destroyer or housing a *miisan-level* AI. We... err liberated her from a storage facility deep in the heart of the empire. They weren't using her, and that's just criminal for a beauty like this."

He stroked the wall soothingly as he spoke. Eris's eyes widened as the hum under her palm changed, becoming more like a contented purr.

"It knows you're here?" It had to. There was no other reason for the reaction.

Zero's lips quirked and he tapped his temple with a metal finger. "Direct uplink. One of the perks of my non-organic nature. Okay... let's take a look at this message of yours. Shall we?"

She nodded, sitting down as the big cyborg held the seat out for her. "I doubt it's anything important. He... I..."

She sighed. "My brother and I don't get along well. I don't know why he's contacted me. Probably just to be an asshole and shout at me."

The console flared to life in front of her although this time instead of Latharian script, code was filling the screen. Okay, so the UI wasn't as friendly down here. Good thing she had Zero with her. She wouldn't have been able to make heads nor tails of it otherwise.

"That's what worries me. Not him shouting at you. Although, if he did and he wasn't your brother, I'd be forced to rip him a new asshole." He slid her a sideways look as he fed the message strip into a data port just under the screen. "That is... unless you *want* me to?"

She snorted. "I've been dealing with my brother since we were in the womb. If there are any new assholes to be ripped, I'm more than capable of doing it myself, but thank you for the offer."

"Okay. Just checking. Offer's there anyhow."

She nodded, watching what he was doing with fascination. What she assumed was the message strip appeared on screen, in wireframe format. Zero moved his hands and the model moved around, spinning so they could look at it from every angle.

"What are you doing?"

"I have it set up in a virtual container within the computer core."

His voice was distracted, with that mechanical inflection that told her his attention was somewhere else. It was the smallest change, so small she doubted many people would pick it up, but... yeah, for some reason she was hypersensitive about anything to do with the big cyborg.

"It's completely self-contained. No way out of the container, and no way off the ship."

"Okay..."

"Which means if opening the message does something it shouldn't—like ping our location, or worse, try and upload an overload sequence to our engine core—we'll see it within the container."

Ah. That made sense. "And it won't be able to actually do those things? It'll just think it has?"

"Bingo." He shot a finger gun at her. "And that will mean it's not a message at all, but a trap. Which means we'll really need to go have a chat with your brother, and I am calling dibs on new asshole ripping."

She chuckled. "If that happens, he's all yours. When do we find out?"

"Now."

Zero moved his hands, and the diagram of the message strip glowed on the screen. It turned around and up and over and then moved to the side, a small screen emerging like a speech bubble. The logo of the comms-service rotated slowly.

"Okay. No pings, no viruses." He frowned. "There's something called a 'read receipt' that wants to send a message back to the stream server?"

"Yeah, that's normal. Ignore it." So her brother really *had* sent her a message. She wondered what he wanted. "How do I play the message?"

"Just tap the screen. You can play it right there in the container just the same as normal."

Reaching out, she tapped the screen and opened the message. The view changed, the logo dissolving to be replaced by her brother's face.

She was used to seeing a smug, arrogant expression on Eric's face but instead, he looked... scared? His gaze darted around him as he spoke, the screen shaking as though he was walking.

"Eris... I don't know if this will get to you," he said, slightly out of breath. That was normal. Eric had never been one for exercising anything other than his brain.

"I don't know who else to turn to. There's... shit, hold on..." He turned the screen, and they had a brief view of a corridor wall and a door. Then they were plunged into darkness. The sounds of a muffled conversation reached them and then heavy footsteps and the sound of a door opening and closing.

"Fuck... that was close." Eric's face reappeared on

screen, pinched and worried. He looked exhausted like he hadn't slept properly in weeks. The room was dark around him but she could make enough out to recognize a lab.

"Eris, this project I'm on... It's not what they said it was. We made a breakthrough and... and... shit. They have a person here, Eris. An alien, I think anyway. She's..." He swallowed, looking like he was about to throw up. "They're experimenting on her. I have to help her. *Do* something, but people who ask questions here disappear and I think they're onto me."

He stopped talking for a second, looking up toward where the door must be. "Shit. They're coming. Please, Eris, you have to help. You have to stop them. I've sent you an encrypted data-pack buried in this message... enough evidence to bury these assholes for good."

The screen flickered as a sequence of numbers overlaid across Eric's face for a second.

"I gotta go. I'm gonna try and get out of this place and go underground. If I don't make it..." His expression altered, self-recrimination in his eyes. "I'm sorry for being a shit brother and an even shittier twin. I should have been there for you. I love you. Okay?"

She sat in stunned silence as the screen went blank, eyes wide as she stared at the screen. The revolving logo returned but she didn't see it. Then her chin lifted.

Never mind about the attempt on her life, her brother was in trouble.

And nothing in creation would stop her from helping him.

14

"Yes... Humans are pricks, what do you think I've been telling you?" Sparky demanded, his arms folded across his chest as he glared around the briefing room.

It was actually the back part of the *Sprite*'s bridge, behind the command and station console. The space allowed just enough room for them all around the holo-table if they didn't mind getting cozy.

"Yeah, well... we didn't think you meant *actual* pricks," T'Raal muttered in self-defense, rubbing at the back of his neck. He still wore a stunned expression after Zero had shown them the data Eric had sent over. Proof of a secret government project, experimenting on an unknown woman.

An unknown *alien* woman.

"Nope. We are, in fact, actual pricks." Sparky barked a hard laugh. "We've been killing each other for thousands of years before we decided strapping ourselves to rockets to go look at the stars was a good idea. And then we just brought all that shittiness with us. How else do you explain that lot on Praxis? Or places like Mirax? If you ask me, the first thing some of us were going to do when we saw an alien was take it apart to see how it worked."

Eris folded her arms, not arguing with Sparky as the two humans looked around the stunned faces of the Warborne. She had nothing to add. Humans as a species were pretty shitty. Usually to each other since the rest of the galaxy seemed to have bigger balls or guns.

"Yeah, but we're not any better. Are we?" Beauty commented. "Look at the *oonat*. We use them as servants or species like the *Ovverta* or the *Seratovians*."

Those were names Eris wasn't familiar with, but the rest of the group reacted with outrage.

"The Ovverta were barbarians!"

"Deserved everything they got!"

"The Seratovians? You'll start talking about the human's Easter hippo next."

"Bunny," she corrected quietly, but it went unheard as everyone looked at Beauty.

He looked back, his arms folded over his chest. As tall as the other Warborne, he was more slender in build, but he had a dangerous edge around him that warned against underestimating him.

His pale blue eyes held a look she'd seen before, on soldiers coming back from war and people who'd survived disasters. The look said he'd seen and done terrible things to survive. She suppressed a shiver. She would never want to cross this man, not unless she wanted to spend the rest of her life looking over her shoulder.

"Regardless, the fact stands. *This...*" He jabbed long fingers at the tabletop to emphasize his point. "Is no worse than shit the Lathar have done. Just take people like Red, for example. It's not her fault her mother was raped by a clutch of Krynassis. Now was it? And did her family support her through it? No, they expected her to get rid of Red when she was born and forget it ever happened. Sorry, Red."

Eris's eyes widened. Shit. She'd had no idea of the woman's history, but that was...

"Crap. Doll, I'm sorry that happened to you." Sparky took the words out of her mouth, his expression unusually serious as he looked over at the Amazonian alien.

"Don't be." Red's reply was brusque and no-nonsense. "And not all Lathar are dicks. Just that group of assholes. Fucking clans, it's all about their name and bloodlines. My mom... was made of stronger stuff. She taught me everything I know."

T'Raal reached out, covering her hand on the side of the tabletop. "She was an amazing woman, Red. Truly missed."

There was definitely history there, but unlike with Fin, Red's relationship with T'Raal seemed more familial in nature.

"So... now we've established we're all as shitty as each other," Beauty pressed on, rubbing at the stubble on his jaw. "What are we going to do about this group of assholes and the woman they're experimenting on. Do we know what species she is, or what condition she's in?"

"Nope. This is all we have from Dr. Archer."

Zero flicked up the data-stream again. It was mostly reports and analysis from Eric's work. She didn't understand most of it. Eric had always been the more cerebral of the two of them. Still, from his spidery notes dotted throughout the data she followed his suspicions about the data source from idle musings through to full-on panic.

"It appears his project is a cover for another one, the Chimera Project. They've been feeding information to several different research projects, but Eric couldn't get information on all of them. Just enough to paint a very unpleasant picture. It looks like they are experimenting on other species to apply genetic advantages to their own DNA."

Red frowned. "That's nothing new. The Lathar have been doing that for countless generations." She nodded toward Fin. "Adaptations like the Navarr have, or stronger bones like Skinny's for heavy-gravity planets. If gossip is right and humanity are a version of Lathar, their DNA is easily alterable. They don't need to experiment on other species for that, just themselves."

Eris sighed and pushed her bangs back off her face. "Yeah... about that. We've got a history of doing that as well."

"Savages," Beauty shook his head. "Well, there's nothing for it. Whoever this female is, we need to go find her... then nuke this place flat as a warning to these assholes not to do it again."

"Shouldn't we inform the Earth government?" Fin broke in.

Everyone turned to look at him, eyebrows raised. He lifted his hands in surrender. "Hey, just playing devil's advocate here. Perhaps we should keep them in the loop, that's all."

"We're a Latharian crew operating behind enemy lines in an area of space under the emperor's personal protection," T'Raal growled. "When would you like your execution scheduled...morning or evening? Because that's what's going to happen the instant anyone finds out we've been here."

Fin shrugged. "Yeah... point taken. Probably best to do this on the down-low."

"If that's the case..." Eris leaned in and altered the holomap in front of them. Turning it on its axis, she highlighted a couple of trade routes. "We can take the Icharus route. When we hit this tri-sun system here, sensors from any other system are compromised. Basically, we can drop off the grid and reappear..." She flipped the map again. "Here. Practically on the doorstep of the moon this lab is supposed to be on. Hopefully, Eric is there and we can nab him at the same time."

T'Raal nodded. "It's further into Terran space than we've ever been, so we'll take your word for it. You and Sparky are familiar with these systems?" He looked up at them.

They both nodded.

"Shipped out of Helios here a few times." She pointed to another system nearby. "Purely military base."

"Yeah, I went through Helios station a time or two," Sparky admitted begrudgingly. "Before they shoved me into Mirax."

"Okay, so yeah. This should be a walk in the park. Looks like a small moon base, mostly scientific staff," she continued, pulling up the plans Eric had included. "Minimal resistance. We should be in and out without too much trouble."

"Perfect. Skinny, plot us a course," T'Raal ordered. "We'll reconvene an hour out and go over the final battle plan. Until then, get some rack time."

He looked up. "That means fuck off out my sight, you 'orrible lot."

There was laughter as the group around the table split up and went their separate ways. But, Zero was a little quiet as they left, pausing her with a big hand on her arm as soon as they were off the bridge.

"I don't want you on the battle team," he said abruptly, his face hard and expressionless.

"*What?* Don't be daft," she laughed, expecting him to be joking. But his expression didn't change.

"We're going into an unknown location with

dubious intelligence. You're already on SO13's watchlist," he insisted, still holding her arm. "What if they've used your brother to draw you out?"

She yanked her arm free. "What? By making up stories about experimentation on aliens? From a brother it's *known* I don't get along with? In case you hadn't realized, Zero, I'm not exactly the white sheep in my family."

His brows snapped together. "Yeah, well. I don't like it. It doesn't make sense. And you were injured. You could get hurt again."

The anger she'd been doing such a good job of keeping under wraps flared, burning the walls she'd kept it contained behind to ashes in the blink of an eye.

"No. It doesn't make sense. You know what else doesn't make sense? Keeping one of the *two* people who actually have a fucking clue how human security forces work off the team. Yeah, you Warborne are good, but I served for *years*. I'm not some delicate little flower you need to protect. I'm more than capable of looking after myself... a fact I thought I'd already proven!"

"Yeah, and in doing so you almost crippled yourself!" he bellowed, the anger in his eyes matching hers. "I will not allow you to put yourself in danger again."

Her eyebrows almost disappeared into her hair. "You? *You* won't allow it? Tell me, when did what I do become *your* decision? When we fucked? Sorry, sunshine, but me letting you shove your cock inside me, good as it was, does not mean I cede all life decisions and control to you. Ever. Now, if you'll get out of my way, I need to speak to Allen about this battle plan."

Shaking with pent up rage, she shoved past him and marched away up the corridor before she could do something she regretted.

Like burst into tears over an asshole man.

Eris didn't return to their quarters that night.

Grumbling under his breath about women and their moods, Zero had gotten ready for bed and tried to sleep. He wasn't too worried about her going and getting herself into trouble. The *Sprite* was a small ship and everyone on board knew she was with him.

She'd probably gone to Red, he reasoned. Who would have offered Eris the spare bunk in her room until she'd calmed down enough to see sense. There was no way she should be heading into combat, not after the kind of major treatment she'd had. He was surprised Talent hadn't raised an objection in the briefing. But... he was still a relatively new member of the crew. Probably didn't want to rock the boat.

He sighed and looked at the underside of the bunk above. The *Sprite* had originally been a troop carrier, so each room had two bunks. Most of the crew used the extra for storage. There were forty-eight rivets in it, he noted idly.

Yeah... Eris would be fine. She'd sleep and then realize he was right. She should leave the combat to him and the Warborne, all of whom were hardier races than humanity. Sparky... well, he liked the human, but the guy was quite frankly insane. If Sparky wanted to hurl himself headlong into danger at the drop of a hat, Zero couldn't do anything about it. The man wasn't Zero's responsibility.

"When we fucked? Sorry, sunshine, but me letting you shove your cock inside me, good as it was..."

Her words came back to haunt him just on the edge of sleep, and he winced at the crude phrasing. They hadn't just fucked. There had been a real connection. He'd felt it all the way down to the soul he wasn't sure he had.

No, he *knew* he had a soul. He had to because otherwise, how had he felt such a connection between them? How had mere *fucking* made him feel so alive and near to heaven? How did her smile and the mere fact she existed make him, a creature who believed in facts and figures, in data and code, believe in the existence of something as intangible as heaven?

But... she'd said it was good. He'd argue it was better than good... but good he could work with. A smile curved his lips as he cheated and used his onboard to trigger a sleep cycle. His last thought as his body went lax and he drifted off was that he would make pancakes again in the morning after Eris came and apologized to him...

"Wake up, Zero! We've got a problem!"

A heavy fist hammering on his door yanked Zero out of sleep abruptly. He gasped and jerked upright, almost slamming his head into the metal panel of the bunk above.

"What the fu...?" He scrubbed at his eyes and checked the time. *Shit.* He'd overslept. They were only ninety minutes out from the moon lab.

"I'm up," he yelled back, opening the door remotely as he tumbled out of bed, reaching for pants at the same time.

"Oh jeez..." Red recoiled. "Underpants, Zero. They're a thing."

"The seams rub," he growled and hauled his combats on over his bare ass.

"Whatever. Nice package," she commented, but without the usual sass and bite. An automatic response. "Get your ass up to the bridge. The humans are gone."

He froze, still shoving his feet into boots, his blood running cold. "What?"

"Humans? You know... kinda small," she waved a hand about shoulder height where Eris came up to on her. "Talk back a lot. Remember them? Yeah? Well, they fucked off in the combat shuttle with a couple of power suits."

"Shit."

Zero finished dressing and reached the bridge in record time to find the rest of the Warborne already assembled. T'Raal's face was grim.

"How? When?" was all Zero could get it together enough to ask.

"An hour ago." The Warborne leader's face was not a happy one. "Somehow they managed to disable the internal alarms and launch without anyone being any the wiser. They took two of the combat power suits from the locker and went dark just after launch."

"So we can't track them?"

T'Raal leaned on the edge of the holo-table and looked up at him, long hair framing his face. "Track the combat shuttle? *Our* combat shuttle?"

Yeah... he knew better than that. The combat shuttle was designed from the nuts and bolts up for stealth insertion. Great. They were completely dark.

Then it hit him. She'd left him. While he'd been wrapped up in happily ever afters in his own head about the morning, Eris had had other plans. He'd told her she wasn't on the team to rescue her brother and she'd taken matters into her own hands.

And why shouldn't she? She was a soldier like him.

"You won't allow it? Tell me, when did what I do become your decision?"

He groaned as the truth hit him like a sledgehammer. He'd cast himself in the role of white knight rescuing the damsel in distress, but she hadn't needed or wanted that. She'd needed a comrade in arms, not a rescuer.

"Shit." He blew out a breath and looked at T'Raal. "Okay, when are we leaving to go after them?"

15

The moon that housed Eric's Lab was so small it didn't even warrant a name, just an identification code.

MD-892-A.

"Charming place, huh?" Sparky asked, his voice loud in her ear as they exited the shuttle airlock. She winced and nudged the volume down with the rocker button near her jaw. The suits they wore... "borrowed" from the *Sprite* just like the shuttle... might have been designed by and for an alien species, but they were so intuitive to use, she might as well have been in her *Scorperio* unit. Well, apart from the lack of bloody big guns.

"Scientists. They don't care much for views. Or anything apart from their work," she commented, her rifle held loosely as they jogged lightly over the surface of the moon toward the lab. The gravity was a fraction of Earth normal, but just enough they could use a loping run.

Designed for low-gravity it would ensure they stuck to the surface and didn't need to use their suit thrusters to stay down. The trick was to glide their feet over the surface, not push. Slamming a foot down would just spin them off into space, which, when they were trying to stay unnoticed, would not be a good thing.

They'd opted to land a couple of clicks away from the lab, concealing the shuttle in a deep valley before covering the rest of the distance on foot in extravehicular activity-suits for two reasons. Trying to land on a top-secret base no one was supposed to know about without clearance? Never a good idea. Trying to land on a top-secret base no one was supposed to know about in an alien combat shuttle? That was an even worse idea.

So they'd dropped in while the base was on the dark side of the moon and its sensors were out of commission. That way, even if they did get spotted, no one could send a message out. Even so, they'd sat for long minutes, monitoring all the comm ranges, just in case.

Not a peep.

No one had seen them. No alarms had been raised. They reached the last rise, crouching in cover to get a look at the lab.

It was nestled in a shallow valley, a sprawling mass of domes and corridors. The larger domes had to be the labs, the largest probably hydroponics to support the environmental systems, and the smaller ones residential. A landing pad with extendable docking arms was just visible on the other side of the domes.

"All quiet on the lunar front," Sparky murmured, his gaze intent on the lab. "Doesn't look like they have any perimeter patrols set."

"It's a lab," she replied, using her helmet's display to zoom in on the nearest section. There was a service airlock not far from them. "What would they be guarding... Lab equipment and reports? Did you see the shit Eric sent? I couldn't read more than one word in three. Made no fucking sense to me whatsoever."

Sparky's lips compressed as he motioned for them to move. "Yeah, a lab that's researching weaponized genetics. Anything that involves weapons usually has way more guards and guns than this. It feels... odd."

"That'll be your suit, pick a smaller size next time." She told him as they ran toward the buildings.

At any moment she expected the nearest dome to sprout point defense canons and cut them down before they could get anywhere near. By the time they reached the relative safety of the nearest building, hidden from view by the curve of the wall, sweat trickled uncomfortably down the hollow of her spine.

"Not my fault these things are cramped in the ol' jewels department," he groused. "Had to go up a size so I didn't squash anything... important."

"I'll squash something important if you don't shut the fuck up," she murmured, slinging her rifle and sliding to her knees by the airlock door. Levering the panel loose with her combat knife, she slid it under her knee to stop it floating off and peered inside.

"Standard mag-seven unit," she said, reaching in. "I can have this open in a few."

"Well, aren't you a dark horse?" Sparky whistled softly as she worked. "Goody two-shoes Chief Archer breaking a mag-seven... I'm impressed."

She chuckled. "Who said I was a goody two-shoes? Don't judge a book by its cover."

The locks on the airlock clunked and switched

from red to green. She quickly replaced the panel and slid her knife away just as the door opened to let them in. It was a close fit with the two of them.

"We need to move fast. This is one of the maintenance locks, so it will show open on a console somewhere, probably in operations." She reached out and patted the wall. "This model is old, prone to false reports. Hopefully, they'll think it's just playing up and check it out on the next rotation."

He nodded, his expression focused as they waited for the cycle to complete. As it did and breathable air poured into the tiny compartment, they cracked their helmets, letting them fold back into the neck of their suits to conserve their air for the way back.

"Let's go in weapons hot, just in case. Eh, doll? Don't fancy getting caught with my pants down, not with just the two of us and no backup."

"Copy that. In, locate Eric and the prisoner, out. Simple," she murmured, bringing her rifle up as the door in front of them opened with a hiss.

She'd half expected the corridor beyond to be filled with commandos armed to the teeth. Instead, it was empty. Deserted. They stepped from the airlock, turning in concert to cover both directions. No one shot at them. No alarms went off.

"Nothing doing," Sparky murmured. "Okay. Going left, heading for the lab. Use this as the RV point if we get split up."

She nodded, but he'd already turned away. Conversation dropped off after that as they made their way through the corridors of the lab facility. Mostly it was deserted, but several of the labs they passed by showed signs of occupation. One had a scientist sitting at what looked like the bastard love child of a microscope and a cannon array. They'd been forced to bend almost double to scuttle by, just in case he should happen to turn around.

Finally, they turned the last corner, the small red dot on her wrist display telling her Eric's lab was just up ahead on the left.

"Easy," Sparky warned as she took point, entering the code that had been in Eric's message. The door slid open in front of them and they stepped inside, Sparky sweeping the corridor outside with his rifle before backing in.

"Lights," she ordered, squinting to try and make out details in the darkness. She should have kept her suit helmet up. It had night sight capability. When the lights began to snap on in sequence, starting at the door, she wished she hadn't bothered.

The lab was trashed. Equipment had been

ransacked and shattered, glass and metal parts were strewn over the counters and floor. She stepped back with a gasp... Blood pooled on the floor and splattered over the countertops and walls.

"Hey, boss," a familiar voice said from the darkness ahead of her. "Good of you to finally join us."

The rest of the lights snapped on to reveal Officer Mills, but not as she remembered him. The happy-go-lucky, charming smile was gone, replaced by a harder, more dangerous expression. Likewise, his station uniform was gone and in its place was the black-on-black combat uniform of SO13—the same uniform the armed men emerging from the darkness behind him wore.

But those details paled into insignificance to the gun he had pressed against her twin's temple.

"What are you doing, Mills?" she barked. "Let him go."

She snapped her rifle to aim at the small patch of skin between Mills' eyebrows with her finger on the trigger. Just one little squeeze. That's all it would take. A slight tightening of the muscles in her hand, as natural as breathing, and her former security officer's brains would decorate the counters behind him.

Her gaze slid downward, to the gun Mills held against Eric's head. Mills' smile broadened.

"Release trigger," Sparky warned in a low voice. He'd taken a few steps to the side as much as the space in the narrow lab would allow, but it wasn't going to be enough. There was no cover. One burst from an assault rifle would take them both out.

"Yeah." Her voice was sharp. Clipped. "I see it."

Shit. She couldn't fire. Rather than pulling the trigger, all Mills had to do to send a bullet through her twin's brains was let go.

"Eris." Eric's face was pale, his voice shaky. "I'm so sorry. I didn—"

"*Shut it.*" Mills shoved his muzzle against Eric's head, and her brother winced. "And keep shut unless you want your sister to see what the inside of that egghead brain looks like."

Eric nodded, tears leaking from the corners of his eyes. He fixed his gaze on her, as though she were the only thing in the room. She understood that response, her expression calm and reassuring as she met his eyes.

"Now we all know where we stand," Mills grinned again, his jovial tone making Eris wish she'd shoved his fucking coffee mug where the sun didn't shine back on the station. "How about you put those rifles down before I have the boys here fill you with more holes than swiss cheese?"

There were too many of them to take on. Eris bit back her growl of frustration and lowered her gun. At Mills' gestures, they both crouched to place their weapons on the floor at the same time. Two troopers moved forward at Mills' nod.

Sparky sighed as he put his hands behind his head. "Swiss cheese, seriously? Mate, if you're going to issue bad-guy-level threats, you really need to up your game."

Mills flicked him a hard glance. "I'll take it under advisement."

"You know… threats of dire punishment, torture, that kind of thing," he continued, not fighting as one of the troopers cuffed him. "Dairy-based threats are so passé."

Eris closed her eyes for a second. This was it. She was going to get killed because of some smart-fucking-alec ex-con who didn't know when to keep his freaking mouth shut.

"*For krath's sake. Shut the fuck up, Sparky!*" The other trooper hauled her around, yanking rip-cuffs tight around her wrists behind her head.

She tried to pull a fast one, holding her wrists parallel rather than over one another. If he'd fallen for it, it would have given her enough room to slip her hands free. His slight grunt of amusement as he forced her hands palm to palm said he was too long in the tooth to fall for it.

"Hey," she muttered, looking up as he forced her to her knees. His blue eyes were amused, but that was it. Beyond the amusement was a chilling coldness that said he would put a bullet between someone's eyes without questioning the order. "Can't blame a gal for trying. Can you?"

"No talking!" Mills ordered harshly, hauling Eric to his feet. "Now me and your brother will be taking our leave. The powers that be want him alive."

He grinned as he pulled the smaller man closer, tapping the muzzle of his handgun against Eric's temple. "Or, rather, they want the knowledge he has in this egghead of his. Kline and Patterson here will be escorting you to your final destination."

"No! She comes with me!" Eric struggled against Mills' hold, managing to break free enough to take a step toward Eris. "I won't give you *anything* without her."

Mills' face hardened and he surged forward to knock Eric to his knees in front of Eris, pressing the gun against the back of his head.

"Now the thing my boss realizes about situations

like this," he said calmly. "Is that accidents happen. Do you want to be an accident, Doctor Archer?"

"It's fine, Eric." Eris smiled as she lied. "Do as they say, and no one will get hurt. Isn't that right, Mills?"

"Your sister is a wise woman, Doctor. Pity things had to go this way..." Mills looked directly at her as he hauled Eric to his feet. Her heart went out to her brother; he was terrified and so out of his depth it was laughable.

"... perhaps in another time and place we could have gone out for that drink... dinner and back to my place. It would have saved me going through hoops to tag that fucking awful takeout coffee."

She sucked a breath in. "It was me. You had a tracker on me all this time?"

Her stomach dropped, a sour taste in her mouth. All this time, she'd put Zero and the rest of the Warborne in danger. All because of her damn coffee addiction.

Mills chuckled. "Of course. We knew the good doctor here was at risk of turning, and with something as important as Prometheus, we couldn't afford that. We had contingencies in place in case he went rogue. Good job we did. No way do we want that information to get out. Now it's all contained, there's no more threat to the program. Now, if you'll excuse us, the good doctor and I have a shuttle to catch."

He turned away, shoving Eric in front of him. The rest of the troop turned to follow, apart from the two behind Eris and Sparky. Kline and Patterson. The fact that Mills had named them was not a good sign. It meant their next "destination" would be their final one. A bullet to the back of the head before being thrown out the nearest airlock... No one would ever find their bodies this far out.

"Oh boy..." Sparky began to chuckle, his face creased with amusement followed by an outright belly laugh. "You *really* think we were stupid enough to come here alone? That we didn't have a backup plan."

Mills froze on the way to the door at the back of the lab, looking over his shoulder. "The shuttle you parked over the rise? Already gone, my friend, along with whoever was in it. Targeted missile strike took care of him as soon as you stepped inside the airlock. We knew you were coming."

Eris closed her eyes. Of course they did. The tracker. Even though the shuttle itself had some kind of stealth tech, they'd have been able to pick up the tracker on her as soon as she stepped out of it.

"Yeah... right. You keep telling yourself that." Sparky winked. "But if I were you, I'd watch over your shoulder for the next... oh, rest of your very short fucking life."

"Yeah, yeah..." Mills scoffed, pushing Eric ahead of him. Her twin turned and twisted, trying to keep her in sight as long as possible. But then they were gone, and it was just her, Sparky and their soon-to-be executioners.

"Well," Sparky drawled. "Since we're alone now... any chance you guys'll take any last requests? Good looking lads like you, I'm sure we can find something... fun to do."

Of all the things Eris had expected from the ex-con, it wasn't for him to hit on the guys about to execute them.

"For fuck's sake, Sparky, have some fucking respect. Would you?" she hissed as the two troopers just laughed and stepped behind them.

"You think I'm interested in these tossers?" he shot back, on his knees next to her. "Sheesh, you never heard of a distraction technique?"

Hands behind her head, she closed her eyes. Shutting him out.

This was it.

Rather than the panic she thought she'd feel, she

had a sense of calm and peace. Of finality. She'd done everything she could, and it still hadn't been enough. They were out of weapons and out of options, so she let it go and let peace wash over her. In a couple of seconds nothing would matter anymore anyway; there was no point for her last moments to be filled with anger and frustration.

So instead she let everything good about her life fill her mind—her military service, where she'd made a difference, the tiny connection with her brother, even forged as it was in the midst of fear and threat... Zero...

Her breath caught on a gasp, a savage ache in the center of her chest.

She would never see Zero again. Never hold him, never feel him hold her. Never see that cheeky smile of his.

Never tell him she loved him...

Fuck, when had that happened? She loved Zero. Loved the big, gruff cyborg with the name full of numbers and letters and the pain in the ass alpha hero bossiness.

Kline cocked his weapon, the sound right by her ear. She steeled herself for the shot. Would she even hear it before the bullet tore through her brain, scrambling the delicate tissues and snuffing her life out in less than a heartbeat?

A tear leaked down the side of her face as she waited for the inevitable.

If she'd believed in any god, she'd pray... her only request just one more moment with Zero....

16

_T_he moon base on MD-892-A was utterly underwhelming.

"Is that it?"

The entire crew were crowded onto the bridge as they approached the moon listed in Eric's information as the location of the lab. It looked like every other moon Zero had ever seen. Nothing special.

Until a flare of bright light illuminated the edge, like a sunrise that was here one moment and gone the next.

"Okay, what the hell was that?" T'Raal demanded, the main view screen focusing in on the flare. Whatever it was had been just over the horizon, so they couldn't see anything now apart from rocks and more rocks.

"Errrr... that *was* our combat shuttle," Beauty informed them as the ship rounded the side of the moon and the rocks gave way to a blasted crater with edges like broken teeth.

Zero's heart stalled in his chest, his hands frozen on the flight controls. Eris and Sparky had been on that shuttle...

"Scanning the remains. No biological matter detected. There was no one on board."

His heart restarted with a painful thump. Just the idea of Eris... gone like that. It shorted his onboard and biological systems in ways he'd never encountered before. It was painful and not convenient, not when it locked up his systems and didn't allow him to think.

Bringing them parallel with the surface, he swung the ship around. The lab was laid out in front of them, a spidery network of domes and leg-like corridors connecting them. There was no armoring, no defenses... he frowned, using his uplink to the *Sprite* to bring the scanners to bear.

"The shot came from a ship on the other side of the base," he recounted for the rest of the bridge crew. "Definitely combat-capable. Rail guns and point defense cannons. There's a scientific vessel there as well, both attached to the base by boarding tubes."

"Okay. It looks like they're getting ready to up and leave then. Chances are they know something's up if they took out the shuttle. We need to get down there. Since we're down a shuttle, it'll have to be a suit drop. Beauty, Red... bridge duties. The rest of you, suit up."

"Hell yeah!" Zero handed off flight control to Beauty's console. He was off the bridge almost before T'Raal had given the order. Sliding down the stair rails on his hands, his feet hit the deck of the staging area and he was half in his suit before the others piled in.

They suited up with quick, economical movements. While the empire might only use power suits in extreme circumstances, they were par for the course for the Warborne. Why refuse to use an advantage because some outdated honor system forbade it? Especially when there were creatures like the Krin out there.

"We go in hard and fast," T'Raal ordered, his voice muffled for a second as he pulled his helmet on. A second later, his voice filtered over suit comms. "Technically, this is an act of war, so I don't want anyone down there getting too good a look at us. Zero, can you block all the security cameras down there?"

Zero nodded, doing up the last zips and latches on his suit, and then turned to check Fin's. Giving his battle partner a thumbs up, he answered T'Raal as Fin returned the favor. No one went ex-atmosphere without double checks, even when they were on the clock. Not unless they wanted to suck cold, hard space.

"As soon as we go boots down, I'll jam everything and its mother," he promised and then grinned. "And as for a good look... I can promise you, they won't be looking at us."

"Good." As usual when they went into action, T'Raal's voice was clipped and professional. Zero hefted the heavy machine gun he preferred—in the suit he couldn't use his arm-mounted gun rig—and turned to face the ramp.

"Dropping ramp in three..." Beauty's voice came over the comm. "Two... one... go!"

They were already running before he finished talking, flinging themselves off the end of the ramp as the *Sprite* flew low and fast over the central part of the lab.

A battle cry broke from Zero's lips as they dropped like stones—armor-clad, heavily armed stones. Parting his feet, he brought his gun to bear as they crashed through the ceiling of the dome below.

Shattered glass and the shriek of environmental alarms surrounded him. His visor was slapped by foliage for a second before he landed heavily in the dirt below.

The rest of the Warborne hit the deck around him, plus one, heavier addition that made Skinny grin behind his helmet visor. "Too fucking right they aren't gonna be looking at us!"

"Stay quiet on comms," T'Raal ordered. "Remember, we're behind enemy lines and not supposed to be here. No one gets left behind to give them any evidence to start a war with. Zero, let's go get your girl."

BOOM!

Eris tensed as the room exploded with blackness and gunfire. But where was the nothingness that was supposed to come after? Her breathing rasped in her ears, and her heart pounded in her throat...

But she was still on her knees with the same bit of metal that had once been part of some sort of lab equipment digging into her skin. Wasn't there supposed to be more bright lights, harps and whatnot?

Two spotlights snapped on, and she winced, pulling her bound hands from behind her head to shield her eyes. If she didn't know better, she'd swear those were the shoulder lights on a *Scorperio*...

"Don't go into the light!" Sparky warbled and then grinned as heavy footsteps brought Skinny and Zero into view from the darkness. Dressed in power suits like the ones she and Sparky had stolen, they both had their helmets down and wore matching grins.

"Someone need a little backup?" Skinny asked as he stepped forward to cut her cuffs off.

She gasped, scrambling to her feet. A second later, she slammed into Zero, almost taking him off his feet as she threw her arms around his neck. He rocked on his feet and smiled.

"Hey, beautiful," he murmured, pressing his forehead against hers.

"Hey," she managed, her throat thick and choked. He'd come for her. Even after their argument and her being mad at him, he'd come to find her. "Zero... listen, I'm so—"

He shushed her up, finger against her lips as he pulled back to look down at her.

"You have nothing to be sorry for." His voice was soft, just between them but she was aware of the rest of the team listening in. And she didn't care. Not one jot.

"I was the one at fault. I see that now. I..." For the first time since she'd met him, he seemed to lose his innate self-confidence. He bit his lip, looking down for a second as if to collect his thoughts... or get them in order.

Then he looked up and the expression in his eyes speared her to the core.

"I should be apologizing... I *am* apologizing..." he corrected himself in a soft voice, cupping her face, his thumb brushing gently over her lips.

"I'm sorry, Eris. I should have listened to you. I shouldn't have told you that you couldn't come. I was scared of losing you. You... you've become too important to me. I can't bear the thought of anything happening to you. That's why I tried to keep you on the ship. I thought if I protected you, kept you safe... I could... I mean... what I'm trying to say is."

"Oh, for fuck's sake. This is agony," Sparky broke

in. "What he's trying to say is that he's a fucking tit and he lo—"

His words were cut off as Skinny wrapped a big arm around his neck and muffled him. The human squeaked, slapping at the bigger man's arm and trying to free himself.

"Sorry, bud, but some things a guy just has to say for himself." Skinny nodded toward Zero to carry on.

"He's right." Zero looked back at her, his expression tortured. "I was an utter idiot. I totally deserve it if you want nothing to do with me anymore. I just... "

"Oh, for heaven's sake," she murmured breathlessly. "Just tell me you love me and kiss me already!"

The smile that broke over his lips rivaled the beauty of any sunrise.

"Yes, ma'am, Chief Archer," he whispered, gathering her closer against him. Bending his head, he brought his lips close enough so they breathed the same air before murmuring against them. "Eris... I love you."

And then he kissed her.

It wasn't like any kiss he'd given her before. It was soft and sweet, heartbreaking in its intensity—a promise and an apology and his heart poured into it all at the same time.

A soft whimper broke from the back of her throat and she pressed closer, needing more. Needing his touch and his strength... and his love. He loved her and nothing else mattered.

Breaking from the kiss breathlessly, she held him close. Looked up into his eyes and saw the rawness there. The insecurity and the need.

"I love you, Zero." Her words were a soft whisper but she knew he heard her. His eyes warmed with emotion and relief, his arms tightening around her. "You're a big lug and you're bossy, but I love you."

"Thank the gods," he whispered. His voice was raw as he crushed her against his broad chest. Trembles ran through his big frame, and she stroked gentle fingertips over the short hair at the nape of his neck.

"I thought I'd completely fucked up, and you wanted nothing more to do with me," he admitted, his voice muffled against her neck. "Or that maybe you would forgive me but want nothing more than sex. Nothing serious."

She gave a soft chuckle. "Well, we can talk about sex later..."

"Not the only people in the room," Sparky

managed to wriggle loose enough from Skinny's hold to remark. "And, in case you guys hadn't realized, we're kind of in the middle of something right now? Like getting the fuck out of here..."

Zero barked a short laugh as he let her go, keeping a hand around her waist as they faced the rest of the team. Warmth filled her as she realized they really had pulled out all the stops to come and rescue her and Sparky. Their own species wanted nothing more than to wipe them out of existence, but the aliens were on their side. She could work with that...

"They have Eric," she gasped, looking at Zero. "They have my brother. They were going to take him somewhere. We have to rescue him."

Zero smiled and turned her around. The spotlights had dimmed a little to reveal it *was* her Scorperio suit. A small pang of jealousy hit her as she flicked a glance up at the darkened visor. Who had they gotten to pilot her? It had to be Red. Although she was taller than Eris, she was the only one of the Warborne who would fit.

"Thought you might need a little something..." Zero whispered by her ear and, as she watched, the front of the suit cracked open in a hiss of clamps and released air to reveal...

Nothing. There was no one piloting it.

"Huh?" she turned to find Zero watching her with a smile curving his lips. He tapped his temple. Her jaw dropped. *He'd* brought it down here for her. Shit, was there anything her man couldn't do?

"I do believe you're improperly dressed," T'Raal added. "But make it quick. Those shuttles were getting ready to leave."

She was out of the Latharian power suit in a heartbeat, Zero stuffing it into a backpack he carried. Slipping into her own suit again was like putting on a well-worn pair of sneakers, only better.

"Welcome, Sergeant Archer," it purred as she slid into the pilot's sling. "Calibrating for your preferences. Please wait... preferences set."

"Thank you," she replied in surprise. It appeared the upgrades Red had made weren't just limited to the outer shell. She'd also done something to the operating system. It was faster and way more responsive than before.

"You're very welcome. Would you like me to engage upper torso systems?"

Her lower body locked into place. She bit her lip as a prickle she'd never thought she would feel again raced along her limbs. The suit was interfacing with her neural implants, but the link was stronger and faster than anything she'd felt before.

She closed her eyes as it hit her. She'd thought her life was over, that she was just a washed-up old veteran, drinking and reliving the glory days while in her cups. That her mother was right and no one would want her anymore unless she got herself fixed.

She'd thought that, deep down, until Zero and the Warborne had come along. They'd made her realize she didn't need fixing. She needed *family*. Not a white knight to come and save her, the role her mother had cast so many would-be suitors into, but someone who saw her as an equal.

A partner. In love and life.

With a smile, she opened her eyes and looked around. Zero smiled at her and Skinny gave her a thumbs up. Even Sparky grinned. Her heart overflowed. Her new family were all around her and that was all she needed.

It would be all she would ever need.

Checking her harness with practiced movements, she slid her arms into the arms of the suit. The clamps wrapped around her arms just above the elbow and then over her wrists as her hands closed around the controls.

"Engage upper torso systems," she confirmed. "Close unit and armor up. Go weapons hot."

The torso folded into place around her, heads-up display live almost immediately.

"Damn, girl," she whistled as she saw the changes. "You're looking *good*. Red did an awesome job with you. Remind me to thank her."

"*Thank you,* Sergeant. Weapons are hot and targeting systems are active."

Eris grinned as she rolled her shoulders and arms. The spotlights snapped off, and the guns on her shoulders rotated in their firing racks, the laser sights tracing a 360 on the walls of the ruined lab. Perfect.

"Ready to rock and roll," she told T'Raal as she turned, heading for the doorway. "Stay behind me and try to keep up."

WATCHING Eris go into combat fully suited up was awe-inspiring. Zero grinned as she barreled through the lab like she was an armored wrecking ball, using the heavy guns mounted on her shoulders and her suit itself. She took out walls and doors, keeping SO13 soldiers off them as they raced toward their objective.

Zero checked the schematics of the base his onboard helpfully showed in the corner of his vision. He merged the feed with the heads-up display from his suit, cycling through covering the flanks and the rear with the rest of the team.

Finally, they reached the last corner and Eris slowed, her hand signal making them all freeze. Then she chuckled, and strode forward, straight around the corner and into a hail of bullets.

"What the fuck?"

"Is that a... tank?"

"Where the fuck did that come from?"

Zero and the rest piled around the corners, taking position around Eris, weapons trained on the small group of SO13 soldiers, a human male in a lab coat in cuffs being dragged along with them.

They froze and winced, squinting and trying to aim despite Eris's spotlights blinding them. The *Scorperio's* guns spat momentarily, and several of them swore as bullets tore through their weapons, yanking them from their grasp.

Zero blinked, surprised and awed. He'd known the targeting system on the suit was excellent, but *dayum...* That was some next-level shooting and then some. He couldn't help a sideways glance at Skinny and a proud grin. That was *his* girl.

"Let him go," Eris ordered, her voice hard and rendered mechanical by the suit's speakers. Rolling her shoulders, she brought all her guns to bear on the small group. "Or…"

There was no need for the "or." Each and every soldier in the group came to the same conclusion at the same time. Their faces paled as they took in the armed group behind Eris.

All bar one. A dark-haired human held a handgun pressed against the neck of the civilian in cuffs. It took him less than a second to recognize both of them. The aggressor in the combat uniform was Mills, the guy he'd let arrest him on the station so he could get closer to Eris.

A plant. SO13 undercover.

Dammit, he should have just snapped the guy's neck when he had the chance. But even as he thought it, he knew it wouldn't have been any good. If it wasn't Mills, it would have just been another face. Another "soldier" with questionable morals and even less honor than a mercenary.

His attention turned to the doctor. Tall and slender, his features were familiar. They were the same as Eris's but written in masculine coding over a larger frame. There was no mistaking them as twins.

"Mills. Put it down or I won't just turn you into

swiss fucking cheese. I'll turn you and your team into fucking jam."

"See!" Sparky called out from the back of the group. "Preserve-based threats are *so* much more impressive. Now I suggest you do as she says. You're out-numbered and out-gunned."

Mills lifted an eyebrow, his expression tight and eyes shining with an edge of desperation. He yanked Eric closer, trying to fold himself behind his human shield.

"Yeah? I count ten of us and only six of you," he shouted. "We can take you."

"Boss..." the trooper to his left murmured. Zero's enhanced hearing picked up his whisper loud and clear. Clicking the tab in his helmet, he broadcast it to the rest of the team. "Did you miss the fact that's a Scorperio? And I dunno what the fuck they are... I've never seen suits or weapons like that before."

"We're your worst fucking nightmare," T'Raal growled, stepping forward to stand next to Eris. As he did, his helmet folded back to reveal his non-human features.

Ok... ay. So much for concealing their presence and not starting an interstellar war then. Zero joined the rest as they all stepped forward, helmets folding down.

"Oh shit, they're those aliens... the Lathar...."

Sparky chuckled. "Some of them are. I'm just the bastard about to fuck up your day because I can."

"We're worse than Lathar." T'Raal grinned. It wasn't a nice expression. It was the kind of expression that prefaced a threat to wipe out your entire family line or cause so much hurt and suffering your ancestors would feel the backlash.

"We're *Warborne*."

"Drop your weapons, *now*," Eris ordered, her voice losing any little hint of humor it held before. It was a tiny difference, but stark. The woman had finally lost her patience. She wouldn't be throwing words next time. She would be throwing bullets.

One by one, the SO13 squad dropped their weapons.

Zero gave a small grunt. Not all humans were stupid then... he *had* begun to wonder.

"Eric," she said, her voice a little softer. "Walk toward us."

The doctor's eyes shifted sideways, as though he were trying to look through his own skull to see what Mills would do. A bead of sweat broke away and rolled down the side of his face. Then he took a step. His feet moved first, the forward momentum rolling up his body, through his knees, his hips and then finally he pulled from Mills' hold.

Zero snapped his rifle up, aiming for the center of Mills' forehead as Eric ran, stumbling toward them.

He scrambled behind Eris, still shaking as he hid in cover. Then he seemed to recall himself, standing up and smoothing his lab coat down, his gaze darting between all the men around him. They all ignored him, allowing him the moment of weakness as they focused on the human soldiers. He had none of Eris's steel or grit. Zero was surprised he wasn't a blubbering wreck.

"The woman. The alien," Eris carried on. "Where is she?"

Most of the soldiers looked blank, shaking their heads and looking at each other in confusion. They didn't know anything. Like mushrooms, grunts were kept in the dark and fed on shit.

But Mills' eyes sparkled with something he quickly suppressed. Shrugging his shoulders, he bent to place his gun on the ground, hands spread as he stood again.

"No idea what you're on about."

The comms sparked and Red's voice filled their ears. "Boss... those shuttles just took off. Want me to follow? I should warn you. Scans are picking up hotspots around the facility."

Sparky sucked in a breath, straightening up in Zero's peripheral vision. "They'll have the place rigged to blow," he said. "We need to get out of here. *Fast.*"

17

"*Move, move, move!*" T'Raal bellowed. "Red, bring that ship down to the landing pad. Now!"

Aware they were against the clock, the team didn't argue, just split and hauled ass. She ushered Eric ahead of her, casting Zero a grateful look as he grabbed her brother, a hard hand around his upper arm, making sure Eric kept up.

"What about them?" Sparky yelled, jerking a finger back over his shoulder at the SO13 soldiers.

"Leave 'em," she yelled. "They're like fucking rats. They'll find their own way off this bloody moon."

"Escape pods. They can use the escape pods," Eric panted, out of breath from being dragged along at break-neck speed. They really were going to have to do something about his fitness levels. The skin between her shoulder blades crawled. They hadn't even had time to get him into a power suit. If they didn't make it before the timers blew, he had no chance.

"What about the alien woman?" Beauty yelled.

"Already gone," Eric gasped. "They shipped her out first."

The Warborne's exit from the station was fast and against the clock. Without any idea of what timers had been set, they ran at top speed, heading right for the landing pads on the other side of the labs.

Eris's heart thundered in her ears as she ran, cycling back around the group to pick up any stragglers if she had to. The threat of the whole place going boom seemed to be sufficient enough incentive. They hit the corridor near the landing pad in time to see the *Sprite* drop into place, all rail guns and PDCs armed and active in case SO13 came back for a last flyby.

They raced toward the extending boarding tunnel as the *Sprite* settled on the pad. She spotted the issue at the same moment as Zero did. There was no way her suit would fit. The boarding tunnel was just too small.

"Make sure he gets on board," she yelled to Zero and turned, breaking away to sprint back the way they'd come.

"Eris!" her brother shouted, trying to shake Zero's hold off and follow her. But the big cyborg quickly controlled her less-than-athletic brother and hauled him off toward the boarding tunnel.

She sprinted for the nearest cargo airlock, the heavy *clunk-clunk-clunk* of her suit's feet loud even to her ears. Scanning locally, she uplinked to the airlock controls and activated it remotely. By the time she reached it, the door was open. Swinging herself around and in, she slapped her other hand over the quick release plate on the control panel.

The airlock was used for cargo, so there weren't any of the same warning protocols for organics as the door slammed down behind her. If she'd been standing in the way, it would have sheared her in two. Its opposite number rose as soon as it was closed, expelling all the air in a whoosh that would have torn her free and sent her tumbling into space if not for the sheer weight of her armor.

Pushing off the back wall, she used the lighter gravity of the moon and her suit thrusters to race across the rocky surface and around the other side of the ship.

"Tank... best get your ass in here now," Red's voice warned in her earpiece. "The others are already aboard, and the lock is cycling. You do not want to be on the surface when those charges go."

Eris nodded even though Red, on the bridge of the alien warship, couldn't see her and dug deeper for more speed. The suit was an absolute dream, more responsive and powerful than she had ever dreamed of, but it still took its cues from her.

"Get that cargo bay door open for me!" She rounded the nose of the *Sprite* at a run, skidding a couple of steps before she got traction with her boots. A plume of air and lights gave her a fix on the door as she surged forward again.

"Doors open. Engines spooling up," Red warned. "Get your ass inside *now!*"

Eris hurled herself forward, stretching full length and using her thrusters just as the ship started to lift off. Her hand caught the edge of the cargo bay doors and she swung herself up and in, sliding across the floor in a clatter of metal meeting armor. Red punched the engines. Eris groaned as the g-forces in the unshielded cargo bay pinned her against the floor. Her head fell to the side. In the strip she could see through the side view shield, the doors had already closed. She smiled and closed her eyes to ride out the rest of the liftoff.

They'd made it. That was all that mattered.

As soon as the thrust cut and Red announced on ship-wide they were safe from the blast zone, Eris levered herself up off the floor and clunked over to the suit's charging cradle. Now the rush of adrenaline had drained from her system, her entire body felt heavy and her ears rang.

With a groan, she cracked the cockpit seals and clambered out, her movements slow. The cradle closed around the suit, a ladder swinging into place, and she sighed with relief. When she saw Red, she was going to damn well kiss that woman.

"*Red!*" Zero's bellow brought her head around. "Tell me she got inside!"

Before she could yell out that she was okay, he appeared at the cargo bay door, almost shunting it from its moorings when it didn't open fast enough for him.

It took him seconds to cross the distance between them and less time to pull her into his arms. The seconds after that were filled with his lips on hers and a kiss that had been far too long in the making. It felt like an eternity since he'd held her, and she melted in his arms, a soft catch of need and pleasure in the back of her throat.

He kissed her like she was the last woman in existence. Like a starving man given his last meal. Like she was the sun, moon and the stars all rolled into one. Like every cliché saying and description... and none of them would be enough. Mere words would never be enough to describe the feeling and emotion that bound them together or the way her heart ached until he was near.

He was the air she needed to breathe, the energy that kept her heart beating and the will she needed to keep going.

He was her everything. And, from the way he kissed her, she was his.

He broke away with a soft growl, his chest heaving and his lips a hairsbreadth from hers. Slowly he opened his eyes and she bit back a groan at the expression there. Heat and desire swirled in the sudden darkness of his eyes. She bit her lip, wanting nothing more than to forget everything and just haul him back to their quarters. Then not emerge for like... a week. Maybe two. Perhaps if she asked nicely, she could get the other crew to drop food off outside their door?

He brushed his lips against the tip of her nose in a tender gesture as he lowered her to her feet. "Much as I'd like to take this straight to our room," he murmured in a low voice, "we have company."

"Uh-huh," she nodded, her arms still looped around his neck. "Hold that thought, though?"

"You betcha," he grinned as he let her go and she stepped around him. Then froze.

Her brother stood a few steps off, his gaze flicking between them. "You're a... you're—"

"Couple? Together?" she said firmly. "Yes."

She watched his expression, waiting for the explosion. Tension hung in the air, cloying and electric. Her shoulders were tight, the muscles in her back rigid. She could see no version of this where her brother didn't give his high-handed opinion on her life and what he thought she should be doing with it. Which probably... definitely didn't include a relationship with the alien cyborg standing behind her.

But the explosion never came. Instead, Eric smiled, flicking a glance over her shoulder at Zero. "I'm pleased for you. I mean... you did find the one man in the whole universe guaranteed to give mother kittens, so good on you. And thank you... for saving me."

He opened his arms. There was no thought, no decision-making process. She just stepped forward and into his bear-hug, returning it like her life depended on it.

"You were awesome," Eric muttered, his voice muffled against her neck. "My sister, the badass."

"Okay," Eris pushed away, dashing at her cheeks with the back of her hand. Neither man mentioned the tears, and they wouldn't, not if they wanted to live anyway.

She smiled, turning around and waving Zero over. "Zero, this is Eric. Eric... Zero."

She held her breath as she watched the two men face each other. They weren't squaring off, not exactly. If they did and it got physical, her brother didn't stand a chance. Not against Zero. Hell, she wasn't sure he'd stand a chance even if he wore her suit. There was a lot more to being the kind of soldier they were than brute strength and armor.

For a moment, she didn't think either of them were going to move. Then Eric stepped forward, his hand outstretched.

"Welcome to the family, Zero," he said with a smile as the bigger man stepped forward to shake his hand. Even in the blood-splattered remains of his lab coat, and having obviously been worked over, he still had enough pride to match Zero look for look.

"Although, I have to give the mandatory warning, even though it's more than obvious you can beat me to a pulp... hurt my sister and I will find a way to end you." He grinned suddenly. "That's if she doesn't get to you first."

Eris coughed, somehow managing to cover the strangled choking sound that had escaped her at Eric's threat.

"Perfectly acceptable," Zero grinned. "Although, to be honest, can I put in a request for you to get to me first? I think I might sustain less damage than if she gets to me."

Eric chuckled. "Yeah, I think you might be right." Then his expression sobered. "So, what happens now?"

Zero let go of his hand, his eyes unfocused for a second.

"Uplink," she mouthed to Eric, who looked fascinated. "He's checking what's going on."

"Exactly," Zero replied and his voice had that richness and awareness that told her he was fully with them. "Boss has called a debriefing later. So that gives us time to get you settled and cleaned up a little. If you'd like to follow us..."

"YOU KNOW," Zero murmured to Eris half an hour later as they left Eric settling into his new quarters. "I think he'll grow on me."

She smiled over her shoulder at him as they headed down the corridor toward their quarters, and the beauty of it hit him like a blaster array. He paused, his heart stuttering in his chest so violently he was forced to direct a query at his onboard for a status report. It came back all clear almost before he'd finished the thought but already he wasn't listening to it.

All that mattered was her... Eris... *his* Eris.

He hadn't missed her words to her brother. She'd said they were together. That they were a couple. No hesitation or prevarication. No looking at him for confirmation. She'd just owned it... and it eased something deep down in his heart.

"Look at me like that again," he murmured, "and we won't reach our room."

Startled, she looked at him again and then her eyes darkened, twinkling with mischief as she stuck out her tongue. The irreverent little display hit him in the center of his chest and he mock-growled, unable to hide his grin at the same time.

Two steps later and he caught her up, turning her in the same move and pinning her up against the wall. He kissed her urgently, bodies pressed tightly as he used his bulk to hold her in place. Parting her lips with a hard sweep of his tongue, he ravaged her mouth, taking what he wanted.

What they both wanted.

She whimpered, a soft moan of desire as she wrapped herself around him. He hardly needed to urge her to wrap her legs around him, sliding a big hand down her thigh to cup her ass.

With a real growl this time, he ground himself against her. She was so tiny and delicate, but so strong at the same time. She was his equal in every way, and he couldn't believe he'd found her.

That she was all his...

Breaking from her lips with a desperate gasp, he kissed along her neck. Hard, biting kisses that made her gasp and grind against him.

"Oh... for fuck's sake, you two. Get a damn room!"

They both jumped at Skinny's voice behind them, Zero automatically covering Eris with his body. She giggled, hiding her face against the side of his neck and his heart felt light at the soft, carefree sound.

"This place is turning into a fucking loveboat," Skinny growled and stomped off, shouting over his shoulder. "At least keep your godsdamn clothes on until you get to your room."

Zero grinned as Eris emerged from her hiding place against his shoulder.

"He's right. We should head to our room," he said softly, reaching up to smooth the loose strand of hair back from her face and tucking it behind her ear.

"Sounds like a plan," she replied, her voice low and intimate. The husky tone in it hit him south of the belt, his cock hard and aching where he pressed up against her. "And, if I recall correctly, *someone* promised to show me how roomy these showers are..."

His grin was slow and filled with heat.

"I did. Didn't I? I'll get right on that."

Pulling her away from the wall, he headed down the corridor toward their room. They had two hours before the debriefing, and he knew exactly how to make best use of that time...

Proving to the woman he loved that she was all he needed. All he'd ever need. He might not know who he was or where he came from. He might have nightmares from a life he couldn't remember. But none of that mattered.

He had Eris. He had his heart... and that was all he needed.

EPILOGUE

"There was no access to the alien female. All we knew was that there was a source for the genetic material. I had to dig around to find out she was even at the same location. A simple look proves that it's not entirely human."

Skinny sat back, his arms folded over his broad chest as he listened to Eris's brother during the debrief. They were gathered at the back of the bridge again, the ship's "briefing area" since the *Sprite* was too small to have any sort of conference room.

There had been a brief discussion about turning the two stern cargo storage compartments on the main deck into a conference room, but that had been nixed when Red moved weights in there. So the area behind the boss's command chair had served dual duty since then.

"A simple look?" Beauty cocked an eyebrow at the human, his stark features illuminated by the lights from the holo-display, currently what looked like a strand of human DNA. "Pretend none of us have advanced-level degrees and talk to us like we're stupid. In fact, don't pretend."

"Hey, you talk for yourself," Skinny snorted. "*Some* of us have an advanced-level education, you know."

Several eyebrows rose as the group turned to look at him.

"*You* have advanced education?" Red's voice echoed the sudden surprise reflected in his comrade's expressions.

His lips quirked. They all saw him as the dumb grunt heavy-worlder. He often cultivated the impression because it meant people underestimated him. All. The. Time.

"Yeah. Got AL certs in agriculture and pharm'ing, including genetic modification," he said, arms still folded. "Family had a farm out on a colony near the Tricerdonian Reach."

Had was the operative word. They'd been dead

so long he had to rely on holos and plasti-images to remember what they looked like.

He nodded toward the display. "This... I recognize. Genetically speaking, humans are one step off the base Lathar coding." He'd never seen Terran DNA before, but he'd seen his own and he could make the leap. His eyes narrowed as he studied the helix rotating slowly in the air in front of them. "It looks Terran in origin, but there are modifications I've never seen before."

"Exactly!" Eric pointed at him, his eyes bright, almost feverish.

He had to admit, the male looked a lot more comfortable now he was cleaned up. Oh, and not terrified out of his mind. That was never a good look on anyone. But Eric's manner had completely changed once he started talking about his work. His nervousness disappeared and he was filled with confidence. Maybe a little arrogance... but given the guy seemed to have as much brain mass as the average Warborne member had muscle mass, perhaps he could be forgiven.

"So... this coding here and here," the scientist continued. "We couldn't work out what it does. A little deeper investigation and we found this..."

He shoved his hands into the display and spread

them, breaking apart the chain on the screen. Skinny and Tal both leaned forward.

"Whoa!" Tal breathed. "Is that... that's a sub-DNA strand. What the fuck is all that there?"

Eric was practically hopping from one foot to the other. "We don't know. That's what's so great about it. This is human DNA but with a completely new section retro-fitted. Whoever this is... they're not human. Not anymore."

"Fuck..." Skinny leaned back. His wrist bracer buzzed an alert at him, but he ignored it in favor of looking at the human scientist. "So that means another new version of the Lathar? Another lost colony?"

Eric shook his head. "No. I don't believe so. We managed to get a section of Latharian DNA and we tracked the changes you guys made to your code... this is not a Latharian alteration—at least not one that is consistent with any change your scientists have made before. This is something new."

The alert buzzed again. He frowned and silenced it. He was logged onto the operations console at the moment, so all shipboard alerts were routed to him. It was probably a bulb gone on the lower decks again. He'd go down and deal with it after this.

"Whoever this person is," Eric continued. "I don't think they're from our reality."

His bracer buzzed again, more strident than before. With a hiss, Skinny looked down at the screen. T'Raal looked over.

"Problem?" he asked.

"Ugh. Movement on the lower deck. Probably picked up some kind of pest while on Tarantus." He pushed off from the wall. "I'll head on down and check it out while you guys figure out where our little friend came from and where she is now. Then we can go fetch her."

With that, he left the bridge, sliding down the ladders to the main deck and heading for the lift. Pausing by engineering, he lifted a fire-axe from the emergency station. He hefted it in his hand as he made his way toward the aft compartments where the readings had originated.

"Okay, you little shit," he murmured as the door slid open. "Come out, come out wherever you are. I got an airlock with your name on it."

Whatever he'd expected, it wasn't movement in the corner of his eye, nor the blinding pain in the back of his head. Agony forced him to his knees. Blood dripped to the deck plate by his hand. A small foot in a delicate slipper graced the edge of his vision.

Then the darkness consumed him...

Thank you so much for reading ALIEN MERCENARY'S HEART!
I hope you loved reading Zero and Eris's story.

The next book in the Warborne Series is ALIEN MERCENARY'S BRIDE!

I appreciate your help in spreading the word, including telling friends. Reviews help readers find new books! Please leave a review on your favorite book site!

SIGN UP TO MINA'S NEWSLETTER!
https://minacarter.com/index.php/newsletter/

ABOUT THE AUTHOR

Mina Carter is a *New York Times & USA Today* bestselling author of romance in many genres. She lives in the UK with her husband, daughter and a bossy cat.

Connect with Mina online at:
minacarter.com

 facebook.com/minacarterauthor
twitter.com/minacarter
instagram.com/minacarter77
bookbub.com/profile/mina-carter

Printed in Poland
by Amazon Fulfillment
Poland Sp. z o.o., Wrocław